Celebrate!

A holiday handbook

Celebrate!

A holiday handbook

for church, home, or school

Patricia Alderdice Senseman
Illustrated by Keith Locke

STANDARD
PUBLISHING

Cincinnati, Ohio

Guidelines for Using Reproducible Pages

You may make copies of the pages so designated for your ministry. Copies must be used for a noncommercial purpose with your program or to promote your program. If you or your organization is not the original purchaser of this material, it is illegal for you to copy these materials.

These guidelines allow you to provide copies of all materials needed by your staff while protecting copyrights for both author and publisher. The Standard Publishing Company continues its commitment to offering reproducible products at affordable prices.

Design by Jansen Design
Illustrated by Keith Locke
Edited by Laura Ring

Library of Congress Cataloging-in-Publication Data
Senseman, Patricia Alderdice.
    Celebrate! : a holiday handbook for church, home, or school / by
Patricia Alderdice Senseman ; illustrated by Keith Locke.
        p. cm.
    Includes indexes.
    ISBN 0-7847-0695-6
    1. Fasts and feasts. 2. Holidays. 3. Family—Prayer-books and devotions—English.
4. Christian education—Activity programs.
I. Title
BV43.S46   1998
263'.9—dc21
                                                        97-49426
                                                          CIP

The Standard Publishing Company, Cincinnati, Ohio
A division of Standex International Corporation
Text © 1998 by Patricia Alderdice Senseman
Art © 1998 by The Standard Publishing Company
All rights reserved
Printed in the United States of America

05 04 03 02 01 00 99 98   5 4 3 2 1

I dedicate this book to my parents,
who taught me
about God, family, holiday traditions, and celebrating.
They delivered God's invitation for my life.

I present it as a gift to my niece, Abby,
the beginning of the next generation.

May we all look forward to the time
when we will celebrate together
at the biggest Party ever.

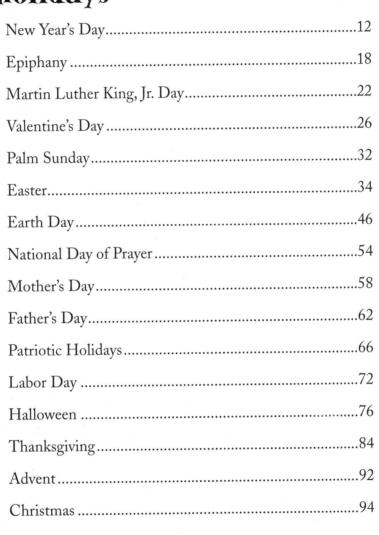

Celebrate!

Celebrate!

Invitations

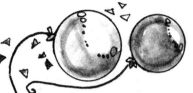 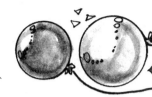

Introduction

God in our lives gives us real cause to celebrate!

Because children love holidays, these special days are a great time to build excitement in studying God's Word and understanding his principles for everyday living. Since the children are already focused on the holiday itself, use this opportunity to examine the holiday from a biblical perspective. This book is designed to help parents and teachers celebrate the major holidays in a meaningful way.

The word holiday comes from two words: holi, meaning "holy" and day. Most of these "holy days" have their roots in some type of religious festival and have evolved away from their original intent.

CELEBRATE! offers more than 300 kid-tested ideas for celebrating the holidays throughout the year. Using inexpensive and easy-to-obtain materials, the practical, simple activities become learning experiences packed with biblical meaning.

These fun and exciting activities can be adapted for use with any age. Preschool children will enjoy celebrating the familiar holidays. Teens and adults will appreciate the symbolic meaning associated with many of the special days they have celebrated for years.

There are several ways to make multiage holiday activities an enjoyable experience for everyone. Parents can work alongside their children. More preparation may be necessary for the younger children. The older children may help the younger ones complete an activity.

At home, school, and church

The holiday activities have been developed so that they can be used spontaneously at home as well as part of a structured curriculum in a classroom setting. Look for these symbols with suggestions of how to adapt the individual activities for use at home or in a classroom.

   idea for adapting an activity at home

   idea for adapting an activity for a class

Families can use this book to build meaningful family traditions that center around God and his Word. Family memories are a significant part of children's lives. What better way to invest in a child's future than to celebrate your faith as a family? *CELEBRATE!* is packed with activities that children and adults can complete together.

Teachers at home, school, and church will find flexible holiday activities to incorporate into a class session. Some activities can be completed in as little as five minutes. Or use the ideas to develop a thematic unit centered around a holiday. Many of the activities integrate other curriculum areas: math, language arts, social studies, and science.

Theme parties

There are ten theme parties included in *CELEBRATE!* Each party plan provides what is needed to have a fun, successful theme party celebrating the holiday. You will find everything from invitations to food, activities to decorations.

The parties can be planned on the holiday itself, a weekend day, a teacher in-service day, or at the end of a class session. Parents can invite other neighborhood children and use the event as a community outreach. Teachers could get together and plan a party for several classes.

The party invitations are designed so that you can print two at a time. One side is printed so that the invitations can be sent as postcards. Simply address and affix a stamp to the blank side. Make sure the paper you choose is heavy enough to meet postal standards. The invitations will also fit an A2 envelope (4 3/8" x 5 3/4"), available in most office supply stores.

You and children of all ages will enjoy using the opportunity each holiday offers to celebrate God. Reclaim these "holy days" as sacred celebrations of God's involvement with his people.

Holidays

Janus, a Roman god, was believed to be the god of beginnings and endings, openings and closings. He was said to have had two faces—one to look to the new year and one to look back at the previous year.

People stay up until midnight on December 31 to see the years from Janus' vantage point. As a matter of fact, January is named after Janus.

The customs of making noise, wearing hats, and having parties on New Year's Eve date back to the Roman festivals celebrating the new year. In ancient times, people made noise at the start of the year to scare away evil spirits. When the Romans accepted Christianity in the fourth century, they began celebrating the arrival of the new year in a different way. They began the year with fasting, praying, and reflecting on their past sins. They vowed to be better people in the coming year. That is how resolutions became a New Year's tradition.

Celebrating a new year is an international holiday. As long as the earth revolves around the sun, people will be celebrating the start of a new year.

Prayer ideas

▶ Ask God for help to meet a resolution.

▶ Tell God about a commitment to a priority.

▶ Promise to work on a character virtue.

▶ Ask God for strength to work on a relationship.

▶ Commit the new year to God.

New

Memory sharing

Invite each person to share a memory from the past year. Suggest telling about one of the following memories.

◆ my most embarrassing moment
◆ my favorite thing about a vacation
◆ God has helped me . . .

Candlelighting service

Provide a candle for each person. The first person will tell something she is looking forward to in the coming year. Then she will light someone else's candle. This will continue until every candle has been lit. Close this time with a short prayer and two or three worship choruses.

 Have a candlelighting service just before midnight on New Year's Eve.

 Pull the shades to darken your classroom. Enjoy lighting candles just before the children go home.

Year's Day

Mumming

Mumming was a New Year's tradition in early America among the English and Swedish immigrants. People in costumes went from house to house presenting a short play, hoping to receive money or food.

Encourage children to write, practice, and perform a simple skit on one of these topics.

- ◆ a New Year's resolution to work on a relationship with God
- ◆ a comical look at last year and the coming year
- ◆ being more like Jesus in the coming year

Invite the children to present their skits on or near New Year's Eve.

Take the children mumming. Ring a neighbor's doorbell. When they come to the door, the children will present their simple skit. Be sure to explain to the children that they are not performing for money or food, as the early American immigrants did. This may be a good time to deliver your holiday treats.

Have the children present their skits during class time or for another class. Encourage the other children to think and talk about their New Year's resolutions.

Rebirthday party

In China, everyone's birthday is celebrated on New Year's Day. Use this opportunity to celebrate everyone's Christian birthday—the day they came to know Jesus as their personal Savior. Have a "rebirth"-day party. Decorate for a birthday party with streamers and balloons. Have a birthday cake made that says "Happy Rebirthday."

New Year's resolutions

New Year's resolutions have a variety of focuses. They can be promises to do good or promises not to sin. They can be personal covenants to improve oneself or to make the world a better place.

Many people make New Year's resolutions and quickly forget them, having no intention of making a change. Use one of these ideas to promote a real resolve to change.

Resolution reminder magnet

Make a resolution reminder magnet to remember a New Year's resolution.

What you need
balloon, noisemaker, party hat, or paper to make a snowflake
adhesive-strip magnets
permanent marker
poster board

What you do
The resolution reminder magnet could be a poster-board shape of a balloon, a snowflake, a noisemaker, or a party hat. Or use an actual balloon, noisemaker, or party hat. Put a balloon cut from a piece of poster board inside the balloon to give it shape. Write the resolution on the item with a permanent marker. Adhere two small magnets on the back of the item. Write "The old has gone. The new has come. 2 Corinthians 5:17" on the reminder. The resolution reminder magnet should be placed where it will be seen often throughout the year—on the refrigerator door, a school locker, or inside a clothes closet.

Airmail balloon release

What you need
balloons
helium tank
curling ribbon or yarn
permanent markers

What you do
Using a permanent marker, write New Year's resolutions on inflated helium balloons. Tie ribbon or yarn to each balloon. Pray that God will give you strength to accomplish this year's goals. Release the balloons as you sing a praise and worship chorus.

Letters

What you need

stationery or notebook paper
envelopes
stamps
pens or pencils

What you do

Guide the children to write letters to themselves. They should state what their New Year's resolutions are, how they plan to accomplish them, and how they will feel about themselves when the resolutions are accomplished. Help them write encouraging statements to themselves: "With God's help, you can do it" or "I know that you can be successful with this resolution." Younger children could draw pictures of their resolutions and dictate letters for someone else to write.

The children then seal their letters in envelopes addressed to themselves. Put the letters someplace where you will find them in six months. Put them with your summer clothes or beach towels so you will come across them in the summer. Mail the letters in June or July to each child.

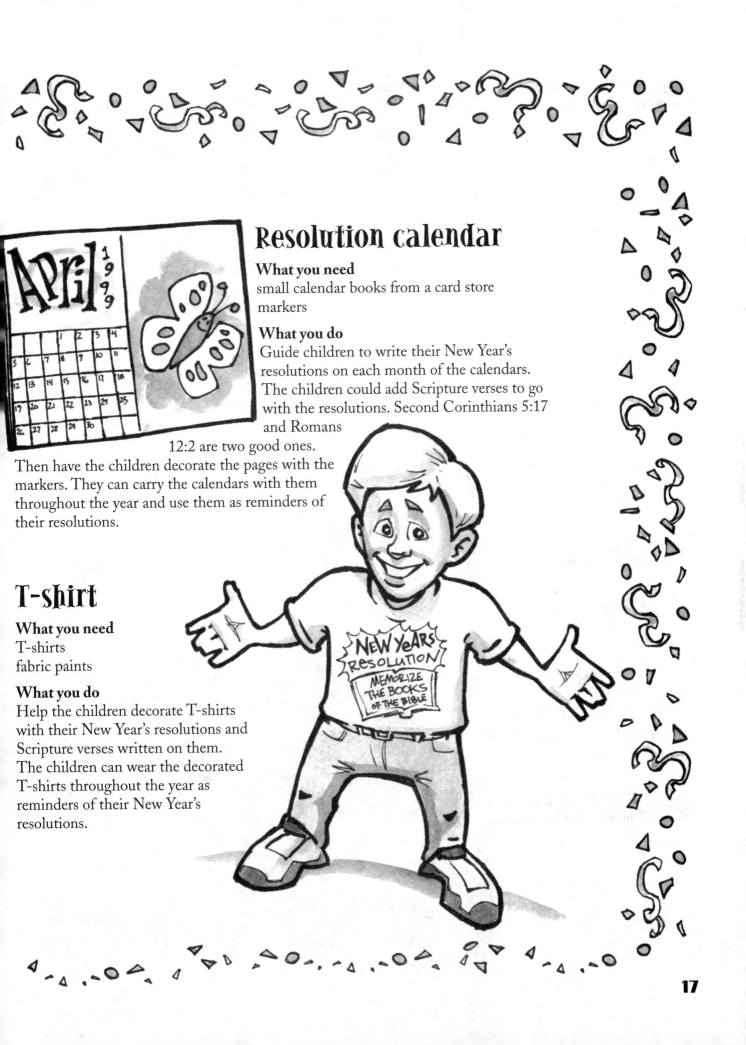

Resolution calendar

What you need

small calendar books from a card store
markers

What you do

Guide children to write their New Year's
resolutions on each month of the calendars.
The children could add Scripture verses to go
with the resolutions. Second Corinthians 5:17
and Romans
12:2 are two good ones.
Then have the children decorate the pages with the
markers. They can carry the calendars with them
throughout the year and use them as reminders of
their resolutions.

T-shirt

What you need

T-shirts
fabric paints

What you do

Help the children decorate T-shirts
with their New Year's resolutions and
Scripture verses written on them.
The children can wear the decorated
T-shirts throughout the year as
reminders of their New Year's
resolutions.

The twelfth day of the Christmas season, January 6, is set aside as the day to remember the Magi visiting Jesus. This day is called Epiphany or Twelfth Night. Epiphany means manifestation and revelation. Some Christians celebrate the twelve days of Christmas from December 25 to January 6.

Did you know . . .
. . . Scripture does not record how many wise men came to worship Jesus, their names, or whether or not they were kings? Psalm 72:10 and Isaiah 49:7 suggest the wise men were kings.
. . . tradition holds that three kings brought three gifts? Balthasar, an Ethiopian king, brought frankincense symbolizing worship. Melchior, an Arabian king, brought gold symbolizing tribute. And Caspar, a Greek king, brought myrrh symbolizing death.

Read the story of the wise men who visited Jesus. Their story is found in Matthew 2:1-12. Act out the visit. Encourage children to think about how these men must have felt. They were probably awed at being in this Child's presence. They may not have fully understood what was taking place. Would they have been afraid? excited? confused? Talk about these various feelings with the children.

▶ Thank God for the gift of Jesus to the world.

▶ Thank God for being king of our lives.

▶ Praise God for being a light in our lives throughout the year.

Epiphany

Crowns for Jesus

To celebrate Epiphany in Europe, children put gold crowns on any figures or pictures of Jesus. Make crowns from yellow construction paper and place them on baby Jesus in the manger scene.

Epiphany cake

Making a special cake for Epiphany is a European tradition. Children will enjoy decorating this Epiphany crown cake.

Make a bundt cake, placing a bean or small plastic prize in the batter. Frost the cake with white frosting. Then decorate the cake like a crown. Pipe yellow icing on the cake to define the crown. Add gumdrops for jewels.

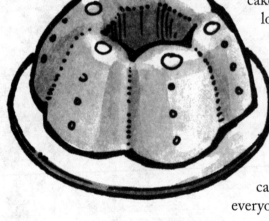

When the cake is cut, whoever receives the bean or prize is the Epiphany queen or king for the day. The queen or king can choose a game for everyone to play.

The apple's star

Cut an apple in half horizontally. The seeds of the apple are arranged in a star pattern. Show the children the star in the apple. Recall that the wise men followed a star that led them to Jesus. Explain that every time they eat apples, they will be reminded of the wise men's visit to Jesus.

 Offer apples as a snack. Cut the apples and discuss the star inside. Let the children eat the apples as you read Matthew 2:1-12 about the kings.

Nativity scene

It is believed that the wise men did not visit Jesus at the manger because it would have taken them many days to travel from their homes to where Jesus was. This can be confusing to children who have seen the wise men in nativity scenes.

During the Christmas season, place the wise men in the same room as the nativity scene, yet removed from it. They could be on a table across the room. On Epiphany, as the Bible story is being read from Matthew 2:1-12, have the children move the wise men to the nativity scene.

The light of the world

As part of your Epiphany celebration, light the four candles in the advent wreath and the Christ candle in the center. As you light these candles, recall their meaning. (See page 92.) Add seven other lit candles in or near the advent wreath. These twelve candles represent the light Jesus brings to our lives all twelve months of the year.

Have the children light the candles as they say the months of the year.

The gifts of the Magi

Discuss the gifts the wise men brought to Jesus.

Frankincense is an ingredient in perfumes made from dried tree resin. It was used in Old Testament times as part of the incense for worship. The frankincense brought to Jesus by the wise men could have symbolized their worship of God's Son.

Although gold is not native to Palestine, it is frequently mentioned in the Bible. It was used to decorate the tabernacle and the temple. The gold brought to Jesus gave tribute to him as the King of kings.

Myrrh is an expensive plant used in perfume and incense. It was also used during Bible times to prepare bodies for burial. The myrrh brought to Jesus reminds us of the death he suffered to pay for our sins.

Gift giving

Some families keep one Christmas present wrapped for each family member until Epiphany. These gifts are exchanged on the twelfth night to remember the gifts given to Jesus by the wise men.

Song ideas

"King of Kings" (Conty and Batya, Maranatha)

"Crown Him With Many Crowns" (Bridges and Thring)

"Victory Chant" (Joseph Vogels, Maranatha)

"Jesus is King" (Churchill, Springtide)

"The Twelve Days of Christmas"

Sing "The Twelve Days of Christmas." Explain this song's connection to Epiphany, the twelfth day after Christmas.

Potpourri sachet

Help children make a potpourri sachet that includes the gifts the wise men gave Jesus.

What you need
netting
lace
gold ribbon
purchased potpourri
measuring cups
scissors
rubber bands
poster board
pens or markers

What you do
Cut 12″ circles from the netting and lace. Lay the netting circle on top of the lace circle. Place 1 cup potpourri in the center of the netting circle. Gather up the edges of the netting and lace circles around the potpourri. Secure with a rubber band. Tie an 18″ length of gold ribbon around the rubber band. Write the following sentence on a 1″ x 3″ piece of poster board: "I worship Jesus, the King of kings, because he died for my sins."

Explain to the children how the potpourri sachet represents the kings' three gifts: the myrrh and frankincense were used for perfumes like the potpourri; the ribbon is gold.

Martin Luther King, Jr. Day honors a man of peace. Martin Luther King, Jr., born on January 15, 1929, was a minister who worked for the equality of all people, especially African Americans. He preached desegregation and equal rights. He wanted all people to live together peaceably. Through peaceful marches, speeches, and sermons, King changed laws and people's perspectives of civil rights. He did not advocate fighting. His message was, "Don't obey unfair laws. But don't fight back!"

Many people reacted to what he said. He was stabbed in Chicago and stoned in New York. But he was persistent.

In 1964, Congress passed the Civil Rights Act. Also in 1964, at the age of 35, King was awarded the Nobel Prize for Peace "for leading the black struggle for equality through nonviolent means." Through his efforts, progress was made in equal education and equal job opportunity for African Americans.

King was shot and killed in Memphis, Tennessee, on April 4, 1968, by a sniper. In 1984, the third Monday in January was established as a national holiday in his honor.

Prayer ideas

- Ask God to point out prejudices in your own life.
- Thank God for creating people with similarities and differences.
- Praise God for Martin Luther King, Jr.'s life.

Martin Luther

A dream for equality

In 1963, Martin Luther King, Jr. led a march in Washington, D.C., where he delivered a now-famous speech. (from Haskins, Jim, *I Have a Dream: The life and words of Martin Luther King, Jr.,* 1992, 76)

I still have a dream. It is a dream deeply rooted in the American dream that one day this nation will rise up and live out the true meaning of its creed—we hold these truths to be self-evident, that all men are created equal.

I have a dream that one day on the red hills of Georgia, sons of former slaves and sons of former slaveowners will be able to sit down together at the table of brotherhood. . . .

I have a dream my four little children will one day live in a nation where they will not be judged by the color of their skin but by the content of their character. I have a dream today!

Ask the children what their dreams for equality are. Give them plenty of time to respond and redirect your conversation as

King, Jr. Day

necessary. Then ask the children what they think God's dream for equality would be.

Help the children make a poster or bulletin board with their answers. The children can cut out clouds from construction paper and glue cotton on the edges. Children can write or draw their answers on the clouds.

Created equal

Help the children brainstorm places they go during the week. Make a list. It should include home, school, friend's house, church, playground, grocery store, and the mall. Then instruct the children to cut out simple shapes from construction paper or poster board to represent most of these places.

Discuss ways that the children can make King's dream of equality for all people a reality in each of these places. List the ways on the cutouts. The children may suggest not judging others unfairly, working harder for peace, and working together cooperatively. Encourage each child to take a cutout and do one thing during the week that represents equality.

Similarities and differences

Use Martin Luther King, Jr. Day as an opportunity to help the children understand and appreciate the similarities and differences among all people. There will always be differences in people's cultures. However, God created all human beings to be equal.

Read Psalm 139:13-16.

Focus the children's attention on the ways they are alike and different from each other: hair, skin, eyes, height, weight, shape. Then help them understand prejudice by discussing these qualities as superior or inferior. Ask such questions as

◆ How are you the same as everyone else?
◆ How are you different?
◆ Are you better than someone who has black hair just because you have brown hair?
◆ Will you be more important if you are tall or short?

Guide the children to see that what is on the outside of a person is superficial. What is important to God, and what needs to be important to us, is what is on the inside.

Equality bracelet

What you need

Embroidery floss in skin-tone colors: off-white, black, peach, brown, beige, tan

What you do

Help the children make friendship bracelets representing all of the races. They can wear the bracelets to remind them that skin color is not important; what is inside is what matters.

The children will probably be familiar with several ways to weave the floss to make a bracelet. If they are not, show them how to braid several colors with knots on each end. The bracelets can be tied on their wrists or ankles.

Overcomers

"We shall overcome" was a phrase commonly used during the historic marches of Martin Luther King, Jr.'s day. Help the children define *overcome* if necessary. Discuss what Jesus overcame for them: sin, the grave, the world, Satan. Then talk about what we can overcome with the help of God: bad thoughts and behaviors, temptations, etc.

Read these "overcome" Scriptures together.

◆ John 16:33
◆ Romans 12:21
◆ 1 John 2:13
◆ 1 John 5:3-5
◆ Revelation 2:7

◆ Revelation 2:17
◆ Revelation 3:5
◆ Revelation 3:21
◆ Revelation 21:7

Freedom that comes from God

Free at last,
free at last,
thank God Almighty,
I'm free at last!

These words from a spiritual are carved on Martin Luther King, Jr.'s headstone. Discuss with the children what the phrases mean.

◆ If King could tell us about being free, what would he say?
◆ What is he free from?
◆ Why does he thank God that he is free?

Help the children look up, read, and discuss these Scriptures about the freedom that comes from God: John 8:32-36; Romans 6:17, 18, 22, 23.

Guide the children in a prayer time, thanking God for the freedom he gives his people.

No one knows exactly how Valentine's Day started. The Romans celebrated a festival called Lupercalia every year on February 15. During this festival, the Romans prayed to Lupercus, their god of the shepherds and flocks, to keep them safe from wolves. When wolves were no longer a threat, the festival became a celebration in honor of Juno, the Roman goddess of love and marriage. Many years later the holiday was combined with the Christian holiday of Saint Valentine.

No one really knows who Saint Valentine was. Church records show at least two men named Valentine.

One legend says that he was a man who helped young soldiers marry when the emperor said soldiers could not marry. The emperor found out and was angry, so he had Valentine put in jail. The Roman children loved Valentine so much that they wrote little notes of encouragement and sent them to him in prison. The notes said they loved and missed him.

The other story tells of a man who was helping Christians when the emperor was persecuting them. He was thrown into prison. He fell in love with the jailer's blind daughter and cured her blindness. The emperor had Valentine beheaded. Before he died, he wrote a love letter to the jailer's daughter. He signed it, "From your Valentine." The date? February 14.

Prayer ideas

- Thank God for the love he has shown us.

- Tell God about a way you can show your love for him by loving someone else.

Valentine's

God's love

Take the opportunity this holiday of love offers to talk about God's love. Use John 3:16 and 1 John 3:16 to focus your thoughts. Emphasize that God loved us enough that he sacrificed his own Son to save us. Because God loves us so much, we need to love each other too.

Love to one in need

Encourage the children to be considerate of someone who is sad or lonely at this time of year. Not everyone has someone with whom they can celebrate Valentines day. And, because of personal circumstances, some may not feel like celebrating love and companionship. Have the children make or send a valentine greeting to someone who may be sad, in pain, or alone. Include Psalm 34:18 on the card.

THE LORD IS CLOSE TO THE BROKENHEARTED

PSALM 34:18

Day

Soap valentine

What you need
heart-shaped hand soaps
netting
ribbon
unlined index cards
paper punch
markers
scissors

What you do
Guide children to wrap each soap in a square piece of netting. Tie a length of ribbon around the netting to hold it in place. Cut heart shapes from the index cards. Write one "Love is . . ." phrase from 1 Corinthians 13:4-8 on one side of the heart. Write a valentine greeting on the other side. Punch a hole in the top of the heart and tie it onto the soap sachet. Encourage the children to give the soap sachets as valentine gifts.

Have the children make several soap sachets and give them to their neighbors on Valentine's Day.

Love is kind

A Valentine's Day service project

Encourage the children to show their love for God by serving someone else. The children could complete a simple service project, like making a meal, shoveling snow, or dusting for someone who could use the help. Have the children make or sign a valentine greeting card for the person. Include a note that reads "We love because God first loved us" or "We are valentines of God."

A valentine for God

As children are writing valentines for their classmates and friends, encourage them to think about what they would say to God on this holiday. Suggest that the children make a valentine for God. Provide construction paper, paper doilies, glue, markers, and scissors.

Conversation with God

Sift through a bag of candy conversation hearts and find phrases that are appropriate for God to say. Give each child or family member a conversation heart. Discuss each phrase as if it were from God to his people. Have each child or family member then pick from a bowl a candy conversation heart that has an appropriate message to respond to God. Have each person say a two- or three-sentence prayer that includes the phrase from the conversation heart. Then everyone can eat the candy hearts.

Valentine Scriptures

Encourage children to add Scriptures about love or hearts to their valentines. Here are some suggestions.

- Deuteronomy 4:29
- Deuteronomy 6:5
- Deuteronomy 10:12, 13
- Psalm 9:1
- Psalm 19:14
- Psalm 51:10
- Psalm 86:11
- Psalm 119:2
- Psalm 119:11
- Psalm 119:112
- Proverbs 3:5, 6
- Matthew 5:8
- Matthew 6:21
- Matthew 22:37-39
- John 3:16
- 1 Corinthians 13:4-8
- 1 Corinthians 13:13
- Ephesians 3:17-19
- Colossians 3:1
- 1 John 3:16
- 1 John 4:7, 8
- Jude 21

MATTHEW 5:8
Blessed are the pure in heart, for they will see God.

PSALM 9:1
I will praise you, O Lord, with all my heart; I will tell of all your wonders.

Biblical role models

One ancient Valentine's Day custom in the church was for boys to draw the names of saints out of an urn. The boys were to act like the saint they drew for that entire year.

Have children draw a Bible person's name from a basket and read from the Bible about that person's life. The children can then pick one characteristic from the Bible person's life to work on throughout the year. Here's a list of some Bible people, where their stories are found, and characteristics from their lives.

Moses	Exodus 33:12-17	Desired to know God
Samuel	1 Samuel 3	Did God's will
David	Acts 13:22	Loved God
Jonah	Jonah 1:1—3:3	Obeyed God
Daniel	Daniel 6:1-23	Stood up for God
John the Baptist	Luke 3:1-6	Told God's message
Mary of Bethany	Luke 10:38-42	Listened to Jesus
Timothy	2 Timothy 3:14-17	Read God's Word

 Have each child research a Bible person and then report to the class.

"Love is . . ." bulletin board

Cover a bulletin board with red paper, pink paper, or Valentine-type wrapping paper. Have children write examples of love on heart-shaped doilies and add them to the bulletin board. Encourage the children to think of acts of kindness that have been shown to them or that they have shown. They could recall such things as "my older brother helped me with my homework" or "I helped Mom do the dishes."

 Have children write on the heart-shaped doilies. Then add the doilies to your refrigerator art for the week.

 Put the bulletin board in the hallway for passersby to see.

Palm

The Sunday before Easter is called Palm Sunday. This holiday is in memory of the day Jesus rode triumphantly into Jerusalem on a donkey colt as the town's people watched and cheered. Some of the people spread their coats and palm branches on the road ahead of Jesus. They sang and shouted, "Hosanna! Praise God! God bless the One who comes in the name of the Lord. Praise to God in Heaven." Jesus was honored as a victorious king. This event is recorded in Matthew 21, Mark 11, Luke 19, and John 12.

Did you know . . .
. . . the palm tree represented the Israelite rulers in the Old Testament? Palm branches were the sign of victory in battle.

Palm Sunday parade

When Jesus entered Jerusalem the last time, his arrival was accompanied with excitement. The people's enthusiasm at seeing Jesus was probably similar to the excitement of a parade today.

Guide the children to plan a Palm Sunday parade. The children can assign parts and act out the triumphal entry. Have them make palms to wave as Jesus goes by. Help the children think of songs that would be appropriate to sing. The children can also read the biblical account to find some phrases to yell.

Palm Sunday songs

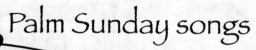

"Hosanna" (Carl Tuttle, Mercy)
"King of Kings" (Conty and Batya, Maranatha)
"Praise the Name of Jesus" (Ron Hicks, Jr., Sparrow)
"Worthy, You Are Worthy" (Moen, Integrity)

Sunday

Palm branch

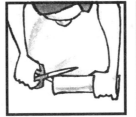
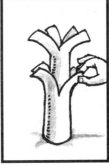

What you need
4 sheets of green copy paper
transparent tape
scissors

What you do
Roll one sheet of paper into a tube. Overlap the next sheet of paper and keep rolling until all 4 sheets are rolled together. Tape one end so the roll stays together. Starting from the untaped end, cut four slits halfway down the length of the paper. Pull the paper from the center to form the fronds of a palm branch.

Parade praises

Guide the children to read these verses of praise. They can then create their own praises to shout during the parade.

- ◆ Psalm 145:3
- ◆ Luke 19:38
- ◆ Psalm 148:13
- ◆ Jude 24, 25
- ◆ Matthew 16:16
- ◆ Revelation 19:6, 7

Easter celebrates Jesus Christ's resurrection from the dead. Easter is celebrated the first Sunday following the first full moon after March 21.

Long before Jesus' death, an ancient festival was celebrated in the spring to honor Eostre, an Anglo-Saxon goddess of light and spring. The term Easter comes from her name. One of the customs of this ancient festival was coloring eggs.

The time period from Ash Wednesday, forty days before Easter, to Easter is referred to as Lent, which means "spring." Lent is celebrated to commemorate Jesus' forty days in the wilderness before he began his ministry. For many people, Lent is a time of prayer and sacrifice.

During the week before Easter there are two other significant holidays—Holy Thursday and Good Friday. Holy Thursday commemorates Jesus' last supper with his disciples. Good Friday is honored in memory of Jesus' death on a cross for the sins of the world. Finally, Resurrection Sunday celebrates Jesus' resurrection from the dead.

Did you know . . .

. . . the tradition of wearing new clothes at Easter time has Christian roots? The early Christian converts who were baptized at Easter were given new white robes to wear for eight days.

. . . an ancient North African tribe had a custom of coloring eggs at Easter time?

Prayer ideas

▶ Praise God for giving his Son so that people can have eternal life.

▶ Thank God that he loved the world enough to send Jesus to die.

▶ Pray for forgiveness of sins and strength to stand against temptation.

Easter

Sins nailed Jesus to the cross

Read 1 Peter 2:24. Discuss sin; define it if necessary. Discuss Jesus' sacrifice on the cross as the act that paid for our sin forever. Guide the children to hammer nails into a block of wood to remember the sins of the world that put Jesus on the cross. The children could name examples of sins or make a list of some of their own sins on slips of paper. Then they could nail the slips of paper onto the block of wood.

Special Easter offering

Judas betrayed Jesus for thirty pieces of silver. By betraying Jesus, Judas showed his lack of commitment to Jesus and demonstrated that money and power were more important to him.

Encourage the children to demonstrate their commitment to Jesus by giving a special offering to the church. Guide them to write a few sentences of commitment to God or Jesus on the inside of a round coffee filter. This could be in the form of a prayer. Have the children place thirty coins in the center of the coffee filter, draw up the filter around the coins, and secure the bag with a piece of twine or jute. This bag of coins can be placed in the offering on Palm Sunday or Easter Sunday morning.

 Gather and give this offering as a family.

Easter caroling

In Europe, caroling is a popular tradition at Easter time as well as at Christmas time. Help the children prepare an Easter hymn to sing. Or guide the children to write an extra verse with a resurrection message for a Christmas hymn. Take the children from house to house caroling.

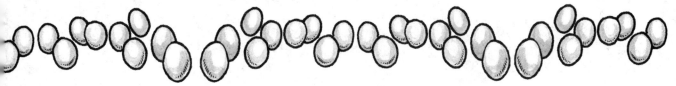

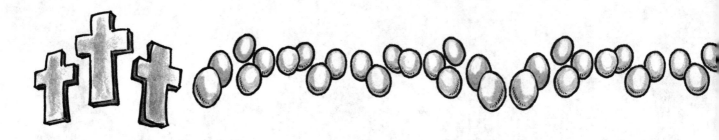

Easter wreath

An Easter wreath is a great way to decorate and deliver the message of Jesus' resurrection.

What you need
grapevine wreath
silk greenery that resembles palm branches
silk lilies
a wooden banner cutout
purple tempera paint
black permanent marker
paintbrushes
silk butterfly
peg-type nails
thin floral wire

What you do
Paint the banner purple. Let it dry. Write a resurrection message on the banner using the black permanent marker. The message could read "He is not here, He is risen"; "He is alive"; or "He is risen."

Arrange some of the greenery and lilies on the grapevine wreath. Wire the banner at the top of the grapevine wreath. Wire the other resurrection symbols around the wreath. The children could think of other symbols to add to the wreath.

Explain the various resurrection symbols as they are being added to the grapevine wreath. The grapevine wreath represents the crown of thorns the soldiers placed on Jesus' head. It symbolizes Jesus' kingship as well as the suffering he endured. The greenery is similar to the palm branches the people used to cover the road when Jesus arrived in Jerusalem. Lilies are symbols of purity and innocence. They are also flowers of peace. The banner is purple because that is the color most associated with royalty. Jesus is the king of our lives. The butterfly is a symbol of the resurrection. The nails are a reminder of the way Jesus died—on a cross for the sins of the world.

 Make the wreath as a family and use it as a front door decoration the two to three weeks before Easter.

 Have each child make a wreath to take home.

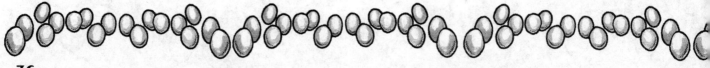

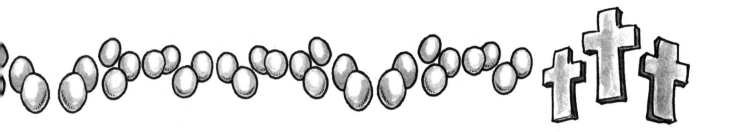

Easter tree

Many families have an Easter tree to display special ornaments designed for this holiday: eggs, bunnies, ducks, and flowers. Help children make an Easter tree with ornaments representing the true meaning of Easter.

What you need
bare tree branch
terra cotta pot
white spray paint
plaster of paris
2 rulers
Spanish moss
various materials for the ornaments
fishing line or nylon thread
ribbon

What you do
Spray paint a bare branch white. Stand the branch end in the terra cotta pot, prop it in place with the 2 rulers, and add prepared plaster of paris. Let the plaster of paris dry. Cover the plaster of paris with Spanish moss.

Help the children design and make ornaments to add to the tree. The ornaments will be symbols representing events of Jesus' last week before his death. Here are some ideas.

◆ palm branch—a small piece of green plant
◆ Judas' betrayal with thirty pieces of silver—a piece of netting around several coins, tied with jute or twine
◆ The soldiers mocking Jesus—a piece of purple fabric
◆ Jesus' crucifixion—a small cross made from twigs and tied together with jute or twine
◆ Jesus' crucifixion—a large nail
◆ Jesus' resurrection—an empty plastic two-part egg
◆ eternal life—a piece of gold foil wrapping paper
◆ Jesus' last supper—a piece of unleavened bread and a plastic communion cup
◆ crown of thorns—a small grapevine wreath

Continued on next page

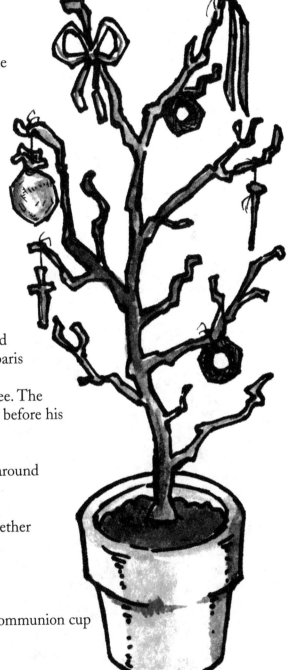

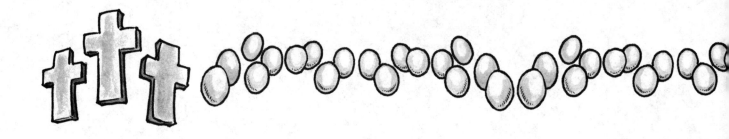

Easter tree continued

Tie the ornaments on the tree branch using fishing line or nylon thread. Randomly add ribbon tied in a bow to some of the branches to add color. Place the tree where everyone will enjoy it.

Have the children think of and construct some of their own ornaments to add to the tree over the years. As the children age, they will be able to put more symbolic types of ornaments on the tree.

Place the tree on your dining room table. Discuss one ornament each day at breakfast or dinner. Read the passage of Scripture that describes the event depicted by the ornament.

Have each child make a set of ornaments. Then they can decorate their own trees at home later.

The legend of the Easter bunny

A poor woman dyed and hid eggs for her children because she did not have money to purchase sweets to give them for Easter. When the children found the eggs, they scared a big rabbit away from where the eggs were hidden. The children thought the rabbit had brought the eggs. The story spread.

Salvation-colored eggs

Color eggs in the colors of salvation. As you color the eggs, read the Scripture references and discuss the symbolism of each color.

- ◆ black represents sin (Romans 3:23; 6:23)
- ◆ red represents Jesus' blood (John 3:16; 1 Peter 2:24)
- ◆ blue represents baptism (Acts 2:38, 39; Romans 6:3, 4)

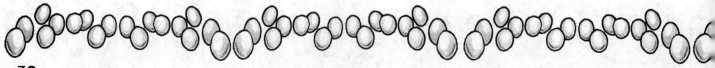

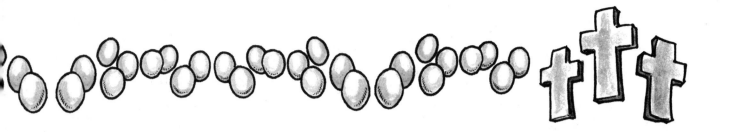

- ◆ white represents purity, cleansing from sin (Psalm 51:7; 1 John 1:7-9)
- ◆ green represents growth as a Christian (Philippians 2:5-16; 1 Peter 2:1, 2; 2 Peter 1:3-8)
- ◆ gold represents heaven, the crown of life (John 14:2, 3; Revelation 2:10)

What you need

eggs
needle
vinegar
food coloring
spoons
wire rack

What you do

Eggs to be colored can be left raw, hard-boiled, or blown.

To hard-boil the eggs, place them in a saucepan. Add enough cold water to cover the eggs. Bring to a boil. Reduce the heat and simmer, covered, for 15 minutes. Drain and cool in cold water.

To blow an egg, make a small hole with a needle in each end of the egg. Insert the needle in one end far enough to break the yolk. Shake the egg to mix the yolk and white. Blow through one hole until the egg shell is empty. Immerse the shell in water and blow the water out of the shell. Bake the shells at 200° for 10 to 15 minutes to dry the egg. The advantage to blown eggs is that they may be kept from year to year.

Add food coloring to several tablespoons of vinegar, one drop at a time, until the desired color is reached. Roll an egg in the vinegar mixture for several seconds. For darker colors, leave the egg in the mixture longer. Mix all of the colors together to get black. Dry the eggs on a wire rack.

Variation: Have the children write the symbol name on the egg with a white crayon before they dye it. When the egg is dyed, the name will appear in the dye.

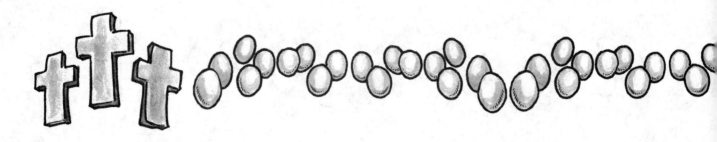

Resurrection message eggs

As the children decorate eggs, have them use white crayons to write resurrection messages on some of the eggs that will be decorated. When dyed, the message will appear on the egg. The children could write "Jesus is risen," "Hosanna," "Jesus is king," "He is alive," or "The tomb is empty."

Easter prayer pretzels

Pretzels were first made by Roman monks in the fifth century and given to the poor at Easter time. The monks prayed with their arms crossed and their hands on their shoulders. When the monks made the pretzels, they shaped them in this prayer posture to remind the people to pray during the Easter season. Turn a pretzel upside down to see the arms folded in prayer.

In several European countries, pretzels are still eaten during Easter celebrations. It has only been in the last 150 years that pretzels have been available throughout the year.

Pretzels also resemble a heart. This shape can be a reminder of the love God showed when Jesus was crucified for the sins of the world.

What you need
bread dough from scratch or frozen bread dough, thawed and separated into individual size pieces; or frozen dinner roll dough, thawed; or refrigerator breadstick dough
1 egg white
1 1/2 tablespoons milk
coarse salt
baking sheet

What you do
Roll the dough into long ropes. Twist the ropes into a pretzel shape and lay them on a greased baking sheet. Let them rise if using dough from scratch or frozen dough. Mix the egg white and milk together and brush each pretzel. Sprinkle with the coarse salt. Bake according to the dough directions.

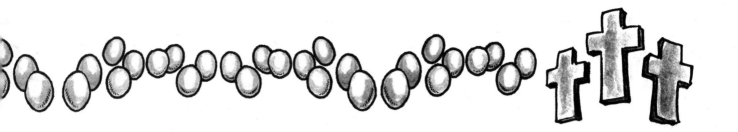

Easter egg hunt

As you hide eggs for an Easter egg hunt, add two-part eggs with these resurrection symbols in them. Once the children have found all the eggs and are investigating their finds, discuss the meaning of each resurrection symbol and the true meaning of Easter.

- ◆ small piece of green plant
  To honor Jesus as a hero, the people placed palm branches on the road as he entered Jerusalem on Palm Sunday.
- ◆ penny
  Jesus was betrayed by Judas for money. Jesus also paid our sin debt with his death.
- ◆ thorn or a piece of grapevine
  Jesus was beaten before he was killed.
- ◆ piece of purple fabric
  The Roman soldiers dressed Jesus in a purple robe and mocked him as a king before they crucified him.
- ◆ small cross
  Jesus was crucified on a cross.

- ◆ nail
  Jesus was nailed to the cross.
- ◆ an empty egg
  Jesus' tomb was empty on Sunday morning because he rose from the dead.
- ◆ piece of gold foil wrapping paper
  Jesus is in heaven getting ready for his people.
- ◆ piece of unleavened bread and plastic communion cup
  With the Lord's Supper, Jesus showed his people how to remember his death.

 Invite children in the neighborhood for an egg hunt. Then discuss the various resurrection symbols.

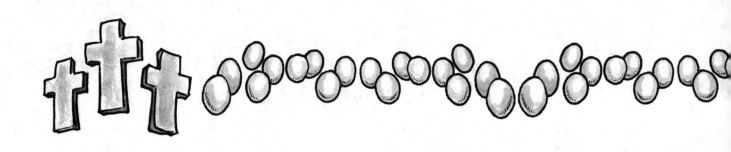

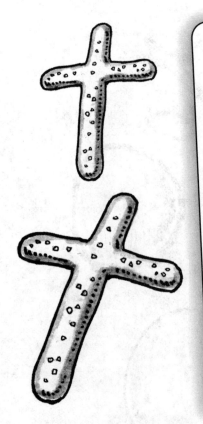

Cross pretzels

In Germany, pretzels are baked in the shape of a cross for Easter. As you help the children make this simple recipe, talk about the importance of Jesus' death on the cross. Share the cross-shaped pretzels and the gospel message with someone who needs to know the real meaning of Easter.

What you need
refrigerated breadstick dough
1 egg white
1 1/2 tablespoons milk
coarse salt
baking sheet

What you do
Cut each breadstick into two pieces—one about 8″ long and the other about 4″ long. Form a cross with each breadstick on the baking sheet. Mix the egg white and milk together and brush each breadstick. Sprinkle with the coarse salt. Bake according to the breadstick directions.

Easter cupcakes

In Russia, Christians bake a cake with the letters XB on it; the letters mean "Christ is risen." Help the children bake and frost cupcakes. With frosting, pipe the letters XB on the frosted cupcakes. When the cupcakes are served, invite the children to explain the meaning.

Hot cross buns

Ancient Anglo-Saxons prepared special baked goods in honor of a goddess. Early Christians did not recognize this practice, so the bakers requested that the buns be blessed and decorated the buns with a cross of frosting. The Christians could distinguish these rolls with their special markings. This became a traditional food for Good Friday.

Guide children to make hot cross buns from dinner rolls. Use frozen roll dough or make dough from scratch. After the rolls are baked, decorate the rolls with an X of vanilla frosting. When the rolls are served, ask the children to explain the meaning of the rolls.

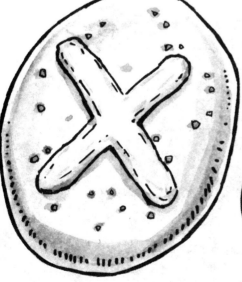
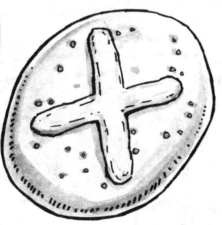
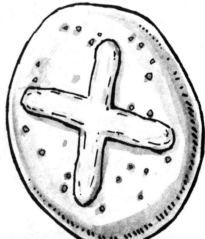

Resurrection surprise rolls

Help children make these special rolls as a reminder that Jesus' tomb was empty on Sunday morning. After the rolls have been baked, cut them open to reveal the surprise—they are empty!

What you need
1 can refrigerator breadstick dough
large marshmallows
spray margarine
1 cup sugar
3 tablespoons cinnamon
baking sheet
wire rack

What you do
Knead and press each breadstick into a flat circle. Place a marshmallow in the center of the circle and pinch the dough around it. Roll the marshmallow-filled rolls into a round ball. Spray the rolls with margarine. Combine the sugar and cinnamon. Sprinkle the rolls with the mixture. Place the rolls on a baking sheet with the pinched edges down. Bake the rolls at 350° for 12 to 15 minutes until brown. Cool on a wire rack.

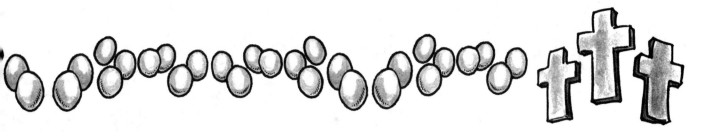

The meaning of matzo

One of the symbols of the Jewish Passover Seder is the unleavened bread. It reminds the Jews of the Israelites who left Egypt so quickly that they did not have time to wait for their bread to rise. They took it with them while it was still flat.

Leaven is what causes bread to rise. Before modern conveniences, a baker would save a small piece of raw bread dough to use as leaven for the next loaf.

Leaven is often used as a symbol for sin in the Bible. Just as a little leaven affects the whole loaf of bread, so sin affects every part of our lives (1 Corinthians 5:6-8).

By eating unleavened bread at the Passover meal, the Jews demonstrate a desire to be cleansed from sin and be devoted totally to God.

Matzo, an unleavened cracker, is used in many Passover Seders today. In order for matzo to be acceptable at Passover, the rabbis require that it be striped and pierced. The holes in the matzo prevent it from rising. The stripes are created in the way the cracker is baked.

The matzo represents a perfect sinless Son of God. Jesus, the Messiah, was striped and pierced as prophesied by Isaiah (Isaiah 53) and Zechariah (Zechariah 12). Jesus was whipped and beaten before he was crucified.

Show the children matzo crackers. They can be purchased in the specialty foods aisle of a grocery store. Discuss how Jesus was striped and pierced before he died. You could use the matzo crackers in a simple communion time, commemorating the sacrifice Jesus made for us on the cross.

Include a communion time during your dinner on Good Friday or Easter Sunday.

Discuss the matzo and have a communion observance on Palm Sunday or Good Friday.

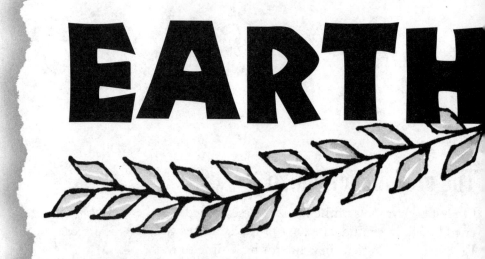

EARTH

Earth Day, celebrated on April 22 each year, recognizes environmental responsibility and stewardship. This holiday emphasizes preserving the earth, conserving natural resources, and reducing garbage. Earth Day grew out of the ecology consciousness of the 1970s.

God's desire has always been for people to take good care of the earth. When God created humans, he gave them directions about their role on the earth (Genesis 1:26-30). Earth Day is a great opportunity to celebrate God's creations and renew a commitment to take good care of what he has given us.

Devotion

Guide the children to discover what God made on each day of creation. Read Genesis 1:1—2:3. Give the children large numbers 1-7 cut from poster board. Have the children write or draw on each number what was created on that day. Then lead the children in a prayer time, thanking God for one thing created on each day.

Prayer ideas

▶ Thank God for some favorite creations.

▶ Ask God to help people remember to take care of the earth.

▶ Tell God one of the things you love about his creations.

▶ Praise God for creating the earth and us.

JOHNNY APPLESEED

Johnny Appleseed was a true friend of the earth. His real name was John Chapman. Born on September 26, 1774, in Massachusetts, he showed the Indians and the early pioneers how to plant and care for apple trees.

Borrow a book about Johnny Appleseed from the library and share it with the children. Make some of these apple recipes to celebrate Earth Day or any day.

⊕ DAY

APPLESAUCE

What you need
1 quart peeled and sliced apples
1 cup water
1/2 cup sugar
1 teaspoon lemon juice
1/4 teaspoon cinnamon
pinch of salt

What you do
Mix all of the ingredients in a saucepan. Cook over medium heat until tender. Mash the apples with a potato masher or mix with an electric mixer. Add more sugar to taste. Refrigerate until chilled.

APPLE-CHEESE BISCUITS

What you need

1/3 cup sugar
1/3 cup finely chopped walnuts
1/2 teaspoon ground cinnamon
1 3/4 cup biscuit baking mix
3/4 cup shredded cheddar cheese
1 medium apple, peeled, cored, and finely chopped
1/3 cup water
1/4 cup margarine, melted

What you do

Combine the sugar, walnuts, and cinnamon. In a separate bowl, combine the biscuit baking mix, cheese, and apple. Add the water and stir until mixed. Divide the dough into 18 pieces and shape each piece into a ball. Roll the balls in the melted margarine and then in the sugar mixture. Arrange in a 9" round baking pan. Bake at 400° for 25 to 30 minutes. Cool for 5 minutes. Remove from the pan and serve warm.

APPLESAUCE BARS

What you need
2 cups all-purpose flour
1 1/2 cups sugar
2 teaspoons baking powder
2 teaspoons ground cinnamon
1 teaspoon baking soda
1/4 teaspoon salt
1/4 teaspoon ground cloves
4 eggs, beaten
16 ounces applesauce
1 cup cooking oil
vanilla or cream cheese prepared frosting

What you do
Combine the flour, sugar, baking powder, cinnamon, baking soda, salt, and cloves. Stir in the eggs, applesauce, and oil until thoroughly combined. Spread the batter in an ungreased 15" x 10" jelly roll pan. Bake at 350° for 25 to 30 minutes. Cool on a wire rack. Frost with vanilla or cream cheese frosting.

CHILLED APPLE SOUP

What you need
2 cups apple cider
1 tablespoon cinnamon red hot candies
6 whole cloves
1 cinnamon stick
1 cup applesauce

What you do
In a small saucepan, combine apple cider, cinnamon red hot candies, cloves, and cinnamon stick. Bring to a boil. Reduce heat, cover, and simmer 20 minutes. Strain cider mixture to remove cloves and cinnamon stick. Stir in applesauce. Cover. Refrigerate until thoroughly chilled.

To serve, stir soup mixture and spoon soup into individual bowls or cups. Makes 5 servings.

RECYCLING FOR GOD'S CREATURES

Help the children make these bird feeders as part of your Earth Day celebration.

 Hang the feeders outside your classroom window for all to enjoy.

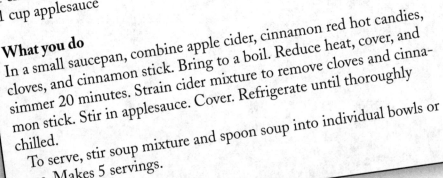

Pinecone bird feeders
Spread peanut butter on a large pinecone. Sprinkle bird seed all over the peanut butter. Hang the pinecone from a tree limb and watch the birds feast.

Bird food garland
Thread popcorn, cranberries, raisins, dried fruit, and bread cubes on a piece of yarn or thread. Drape on a tree like a garland.

CHURCH RECYCLING DRIVE

Organize the children to sponsor a church-wide project of gathering recycled supplies for the children's department. The children could gather and organize common household items that the children's classes use. The church teachers will appreciate being able to go to a supply closet to retrieve these supplies for their lessons rather than having to collect the items slowly themselves. The children could design a flier for the Sunday bulletin listing the household items they would like to have donated. Guide the children to decorate large cardboard boxes to hold the items and place the boxes at the church building entrances on several Sunday mornings. Poll the church teachers for a list of the supplies they use often. Here are several items the children could collect.

- boxes
- small jewelry boxes
- egg cartons
- milk cartons and jugs
- plastic berry baskets
- cardboard tubes
- salt and oatmeal boxes
- old magazines and catalogs
- plastic foam meat trays
- fabric scraps
- trim scraps
- glass jars
- plastic containers and bottles
- 2-liter bottles
- aluminum cans
- nylon stockings
- canceled stamps
- cereal boxes

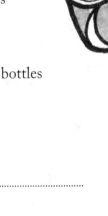
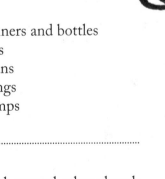

 Work with several other church families to complete a service project.

RECYCLE FOR GOD

Write one of these Scriptures on your recycling container or your curbside bin with a permanent marker or fabric slick paint. Encourage the children to read the Scripture every time they put a recyclable item in the bin.

◆ "Work at it with all your heart, as working for the Lord." Colossians 3:23
◆ "All things were created by him and for him." Colossians 1:16

CRAYON RECYCLING

What you need
old crayons with the paper removed
saucepan or double boiler
mini-tart paper liners
mini-tart baking trays

What you do
Melt the old crayons one color at a time in a saucepan or a double boiler over low heat. Pour the melted crayons into paper-lined mini-tart trays. Cool. Remove the mini-tart paper liners.

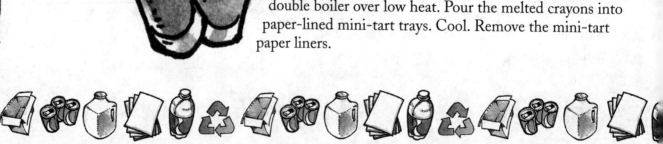

PICK A WAY TO REDUCE, REUSE, RECYCLE

Have the children list ways to reduce, reuse, or recycle on slips of paper. Children will have lots of ideas from school information. Then have them draw one slip of paper to complete for a week. Allow the children to pick a second activity if the first one is not something they will complete. Here are a few ideas for recycling, reusing, and reducing activities.

- stop junk mail
- recharge batteries
- avoid plastic foam products
- garden organically
- recycle motor oil
- turn off water when brushing teeth
- turn off lights
- compost
- don't bag grass clippings
- use cloth diapers
- recycle aluminum, plastic, glass, and paper
- buy recycled items
- carpool
- use cloths rather than paper towels
- turn down the water heater
- dispose of paint properly
- ask for plastic grocery bags and return them to grocery store
- install a low-flow shower head
- reuse or recycle newspapers
- buy in bulk
- plant a tree

 Pick one activity to complete as a family.

History

As early as the First Continental Congress, civic prayers have been offered and national days of prayer have been observed. Congress President John Hancock signed a congressional order on July 12, 1775, which established the first day of prayer for this new nation. In 1952, Congress unanimously passed a joint resolution, signed by President Harry Truman, establishing the annual National Day of Prayer. This law was amended in 1988 and signed by President Ronald Reagan, permanently setting the first Thursday in May as the National Day of Prayer. On this day, Christians all across America pray for the nation and its leaders. This is a great opportunity to focus children's attention on prayer.

Things to do

Plan a prayer time before school to pray for the nation.

Wear Christian T-shirts and jewelry.

Write local, state, and national government leaders to tell them you prayed for them.

Information

Contact the National Day of Prayer website for more information at LeSEA.com/ndp

or write the national office at:
National Day of Prayer
P.O. Box 15616
Colorado Springs, CO 80935-5616

or call:
1-800-444-8828.

Prayer stations

Encourage the children to plan a special prayer time. They will set up at least three places to pray with three different focuses. The children can pick from the ideas below or develop their own prayer focuses. Have the children make a simple poster-board sign with directions for each station.

- ◆ Pray for the country.
- ◆ Pray for themselves.
- ◆ Pray for each other.
- ◆ Pray for their families.
- ◆ Praise God for what he has done for us.

When it is time, the children can be divided into three groups. One group will start at each station. Set a kitchen timer for about five minutes. When the timer sounds, the groups can move to another station.

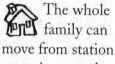 The whole family can move from station to station together.

Set up the stations in various rooms of the house.

Encourage the children to invite family members and friends to this special prayer time.

Day of Prayer

Progressive prayer walk

Plan a prayer walk for the children. Go to several locations and pray for the activity that takes place at that location. Walk or drive from location to location. For instance, go to a neighborhood school and pray that the children will learn, witness to their classmates, and resist Satan's temptations. Encourage the children to pray at each location. Some good locations to include in your prayer walk are a church, school, government building, home, park, ballfield, backyard, YMCA, or library. Tailor the prayer walk to the children's interests and activities.

Picture prayer journal

Make a prayer journal with photographs and room to write. Use the journal to track requests and answers to prayer.

Gather snapshots of family members and friends. Glue a photograph on every other page of a blank book. Blank books can be purchased at bookstores, discount department stores, and some card shops. Write headings on the two pages below each photograph. You could use any of these headings or think of some of your own.

◆ Requests
◆ Answers
◆ Thanksgivings

Add a Scripture about prayer to each page.

The outline of each person's hand could be drawn on the page also. Then you could "hold hands" with the person as you pray.

 Put the prayer journal on the kitchen table, the family room coffee table, or in the bathroom. Encourage each family member to pick it up, pray, and add to the journal.

 Have the children make journals for each of their families.

Prayer pretzels

Pretzels were first made by Roman monks. The monks prayed with their arms crossed and their hands on their shoulders. When the monks made the pretzels for the poor, they shaped them in this prayer posture to remind the people to pray.

Turn a pretzel upside down to see the arms folded in prayer. Make or buy large pretzels to help celebrate the National Day of Prayer. A pretzel recipe is on page 40. Or purchase large pretzels in the frozen food section of the supermarket.

The Lord's Prayer

Encourage the children to pray the Lord's Prayer in their own words. Begin by reading Jesus' prayer from Matthew 6:9-13. Phrase by phrase, discuss the prayer. Guide the children to think of how they would say each phrase if they were to pray it today. Help them rewrite the prayer using their words. Here are some suggestions for each phrase's wording.

Our Father which art in heaven,
Hallowed be thy name.
Thy kingdom come.
Thy will be done in earth, as it
    is in heaven.
Give us this day our daily bread.
And forgive us our debts,
    as we forgive our debtors.
And lead us not into temptation,
    but deliver us from evil:
For thine is the kingdom, and the
    power, and the glory, for ever.
    Amen.
(*King James Version*)

Dear God,
You are holy.
You are my King.
I want to obey you.

Please meet my daily needs.
Forgive my sins and help me to forgive
    others.
Help me to be strong when I am tempted.

I praise you and love you. Amen.

Mother's

Mother's Day was first celebrated in 1907 to honor mothers. Miss Anna Jarvis from Philadelphia is noted as the founder of Mother's Day. She asked a Grafton, West Virginia church to have a special service for mothers on the second anniversary of her mother's death. Now celebrated on the second Sunday in May, Mother's Day became a recognized holiday in the United States in 1914. Traditionally, people wear a red or pink carnation if their mothers are living, or a white carnation if they are dead.

A letter to God

Guide the children to write letters to God about their mothers. The children can use pretty floral or pastel stationery for their letters. Encourage them to write what they like about their moms, what their moms do for them, and why they are glad they have their mothers. They can thank God that he gave them moms who love them and care for them.

Once the letters have been written, the children can read them during a prayer time. Then they can give the letters to their mothers.

Mother's theater

Have the children read Proverbs 31:10-31 about a godly woman. Guide the children to think about ways their moms are Proverbs 31 women. Help the children make a list including specific situations from their moms' lives.

Guide the children to write and act out a short skit about their moms. The children can portray their mothers in the situations they listed.

The skit could be arranged in the order of the verses in Proverbs 31. During the skit, the verse could be read, then the children would act out how their mothers are like the description in that particular verse.

Invite the mothers and families to see the children's play.

Day

Breakfast for mom

Help the children make breakfast for their mothers. Use these ideas to make the meal different and special for the moms.

Secret message toast

Have the children write messages on slices of bread using Q-tips and milk. Then toast the bread. When the bread is toasted, the message will appear on the toast. The children could write "I love you," "Happy Mom's Day," or "You're great."

A love note

Each child could write a note to his mother and put it at the place setting or on the bed tray for her to discover.

Shaped eggs

Guide the children to scramble or fry eggs inside metal cookie cutters in a frying pan. Use cookie cutters shaped as hearts, flowers, butterflies, or stars.

Fruit parfait

Help the children layer fruit pieces in parfait or stemmed glasses. Whipped cream could be put between the layers and on top. Top the fruit parfaits off with cherries.

Table setting

Have the children make place mats covered with clear Con-Tact paper or napkin rings for their moms' special meal.

Biblical moms

Guide the children to discuss moms whose stories are told in the Bible. Challenge them to think of Bible mothers and the characteristics that make them examples of good moms. Include the following women in your discussion.

- Hannah
- Noah's wife
- Moses' mom
- Mary
- Elizabeth
- Eunice and Lois

Greeting card pin

Help the children make these simple jewelry pins to give to their mothers for Mother's Day.

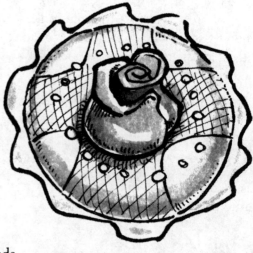

What you need
greeting cards
poster board
all-purpose glue
scissors
pin clasp
clear nail polish
various decorations: glitter, sequins, lace, small beads

What you do
Cut out designs from a greeting card. Glue the design on a piece of poster board. Two or three designs can be overlapped to make a more intricate design. Let dry.

Cut around the perimeter of the design so that the poster board is not showing. Glue a pin clasp to the back of the jewelry pin. Put two to three coats of clear nail polish on the front of the pin, allowing the coats to dry completely.

Decorate the pin with glitter, sequins, lace, or small beads. Let dry overnight.

Help the children wrap the jewelry pins in tissue paper and place them in small jewelry boxes. Then have them wrap the boxes in pretty gift wrap or place them in gift bags to give to their mothers on Mother's Day.

God's gift

Guide the children to wrap small, empty jewelry boxes with floral gift paper. Add tiny bows and tags that read "Moms are a gift from God." Encourage the children to give the little gifts to their mothers. The children could add adhesive-backed magnet strips to the bottom of the gifts to make them into refrigerator magnets.

Pressed flower framed picture

What you need

fresh flowers and leaves
old telephone book
several encyclopedia volumes or a couple of bricks
frame with glass
mat board or poster board cut to fit frame
craft glue
toothpick
pen or marker
stationery or decorative paper

Flowers that press well

violets
anemones
lilies of the valley
bleeding hearts
primroses
baby's breath
forget-me-nots
dogwood blossoms
roses (pull petals apart, press individually, then assemble on the paper)
wildflowers

What you do

Pick fresh flowers and some leaves. The best time to pick flowers for pressing is in the late morning. Put the flowers and leaves in the old telephone book immediately. Position them with the blossoms near the binding and the stems toward the outer edge of the book. Place several encyclopedia volumes or a couple of bricks on the telephone book. Leave alone for two weeks.

Position the pressed flowers and leaves on the mat board or poster board. Trim stems as necessary. Reposition them until the picture is the way you want it. Leave space at the bottom for a Scripture verse. Or add a piece of stationery or decorative paper across the bottom over the flower stems. Put spots of glue on the flowers and leaves with a toothpick. Adhere them to the mat board or poster board. Let the glue dry overnight.

Add a Scripture verse or a piece of stationery with the Scripture verse on it to the picture. Let the glue dry.

Assemble the frame.

Scripture verses to add to the picture could be Proverbs 22:6, 31:28, 31:29, or Exodus 20:12.

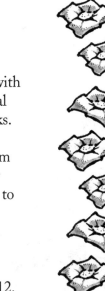

History

Father's Day is celebrated on the third Sunday in June. This holiday is believed to have begun in June 1910, when Louise Smart Dodd of Spokane, Washington, wanted to honor her own father. She asked people in her congregation to wear a red rose if their fathers were living or a white rose if they were dead.

A letter to God

Guide the children to write letters to God about their fathers. Encourage them to write what they like about their dads, what their dads do for them, and why they are glad they have their fathers. They can thank God that he gave them dads who love them and care for them.

Once the letters have been written, the children can read them during a prayer time. Then they can give the letters to their fathers.

FATHER'S THEATER

Have the children read the following Scripture passages about godly characteristics.

◆ Matthew 5:3-10
◆ 1 Corinthians 13:4-8
◆ Galatians 5:22, 23
◆ 2 Peter 1:5-7

Guide the children to think about ways their dads demonstrate these godly characteristics. Make a list including specific situations from their dads' lives.

Guide the children to write and act out a short skit about their dads. The children can portray their fathers in the situations they listed.

Invite the fathers and families to see the children's play.

A HEAVENLY FATHER

Many children do not have ongoing relationships with their fathers. This may be an especially difficult holiday for them.

Help all the children to see God's role as a Father by reading these Scripture passages together: Matthew 6:25-27; Luke 15:11-32; John 14:1-4.

DAY

BIBLICAL DADS

Guide the children to discuss dads whose stories are told in the Bible. Challenge them to think of Bible fathers and the characteristics that make them examples of good dads. Include the following men in your discussion.

- ◆ Abraham
- ◆ Moses
- ◆ Noah
- ◆ Joseph

A MEAL FOR DAD

Encourage the children to fix a simple meal for their fathers. They could fix a submarine sandwich or do something as simple as ordering a pizza with Dad's favorite toppings. The children could help fix his favorite dessert.

Encourage the children to make special place mats for their dads, write notes to leave at their dads' dinner plates, and wait on their fathers during the meal.

A GIFT FOR DAD

Help children make these simple fire starters to give their fathers or grandfathers. The dads can use the fire starters on charcoal grills or campfires in the summer and in fireplaces during the winter.

What you need
paraffin wax
lint from the clothes dryer
cardboard egg cartons
scissors

What you do
Fill each section of the egg carton with dryer lint. Melt the wax in a double boiler over medium heat. Pour the wax over the dryer lint. Let cool. Cut the egg carton sections apart.

HOMEMADE RECIPES

Encourage the children to try one of these recipes to celebrate Father's Day. The children could make the ice cream or peanut butter for their dads. Or the children could make the recipes with their fathers.

HOMEMADE ICE CREAM

What you need

1 gallon coffee can and lid
1 large bucket
1 egg
1/2 cup honey
1 cup milk
1/2 cup cream

1 teaspoon vanilla
salt
rock salt
crushed ice
large spoon

What you do

In the coffee can, beat the egg and honey. Add the milk, cream, vanilla, and a dash of salt. Cover the can with the lid. Put a layer of ice in the bucket. Sprinkle 2 tablespoons of rock salt on the ice. Place the coffee can in the bucket. Pack more salt and ice around the sides of the coffee can. Pack to the top of the can. Remove the coffee can lid. Take turns stirring the ice cream with the spoon. Allow the can to turn also. It will take 15 to 30 minutes for the ice cream to freeze. Harder ice cream can be made by putting the coffee can in the freezer for an hour after stirring it to freezing.

HOMEMADE PEANUT BUTTER

What you need

unshelled peanuts
corn oil
blender

What you do

Shell the peanuts but leave the brown skin on. Blend the peanuts until the desired consistency is reached. Blend less for crunchy peanut butter and more for smoother peanut butter. Add enough corn oil to moisten the mixture. Spread on bread, crackers, celery, or bananas.

PUZZLE PICTURE FRAME

Using simple materials, children can make memory holders for their fathers.

What you need
old puzzle pieces
various colors of paint (spray paint works well)
craft glue
cardboard (notebook backs work well)
overhead transparencies
shellac
family photographs trimmed to 5" x 3 1/2"
magnetic strips (optional)
scissors

What you do
Help the children paint the old puzzle pieces. The pieces look best if painted several colors. Spray paint will work well on the pieces. Let dry.

Cut two pieces of cardboard 6" x 4 1/2" for each frame. Cut a rectangle 4 1/2" x 3" out of the center of one piece, creating a frame outline 1 1/2" wide. This is the front of the frame.

Glue the painted puzzle pieces on one side of the cardboard frame front. The pieces can overlap. Let dry.

Spray or paint with shellac. Let dry.

Glue only the edges of three sides of the frame front to the other piece of cardboard.

Cut a piece of overhead transparency 5" x 3 1/2". Slide it into the open end of the frame. Insert the photograph between the frame back and the transparency.

Add magnetic strips or a simple easel to the frame back.

The children can wrap the frames and give them to their fathers for their offices, dressers, toolboxes, or refrigerators.

There are several holidays that celebrate special national events or people.

In 1492, Christopher Columbus, an Italian explorer, sailed across an ocean and brought back news about a new continent. We honor his special place in American history on Columbus Day, October 12 (usually celebrated on the second Monday in October).

Many Europeans came to this new continent. The kings of Europe tried to claim this America as their territory. In 1776, the American colonists fought the British and became an independent country. We celebrate the United States' independence on Independence Day, July 4.

We honor two of this country's most renowned presidents, George Washington and Abraham Lincoln, on Presidents' Day, the third Monday in February.

Armed Forces Day is celebrated on the third Saturday in May to honor the army, naval, and air forces of the United States.

Memorial Day, celebrated the last Monday in May, originally commemorated all those who had given their lives in defense of this country. Today people honor anyone who has died.

Veterans Day is observed on November 11 to honor American veterans.

Even the United States flag is honored on Flag Day, June 14, every year.

Patriotic

The American flag

When the American flag was developed by George Washington and some of his colleagues, it was designed to represent what the new country stood for. The stars are from heaven, symbolizing a nation built under God's principles. The color red was chosen because it is also in the flag of England, the mother country. The white stripes were added in the red to represent this new country's separation from England. The colors of the American flag also have other significance. Red stands for courage; white for purity and innocence; and blue for justice, vigilance, and perseverance.

Photocopy page 68 for each child. Guide the children to look up the Scripture references on the flag. Read the verses and discuss each topic. When the children have looked up all of the verses, they can color and display their flags.

 Create a bulletin board for the children's flags.

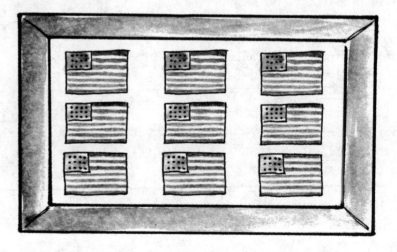

Holidays

The Christian flag

Charles Overton developed the Christian flag in 1897. Most of the flag is white, which represents peace and purity. The blue on the flag represents faith. And the red cross represents Jesus' death on the cross.

Photocopy page 69 for each child. Guide the children to look up the Scripture references on the flag. Read the verses and discuss each topic. When the children have looked up all of the verses, they can color and display their flags.

Patriotic songs

Many of America's patriotic songs have religious histories. Guide the children to research the histories of their favorite patriotic songs. Have the children make reports about individual songs. The children can read the reports and then sing the songs from memory to celebrate one of the American holidays.

The seal of the United States

The seal of the United States pictures an eagle holding an olive branch and arrows. The eagle is the national bird. The olive branch is a symbol of peace. The arrows represent the Americans who are willing to defend what this country stands for—freedom for all men and women.

Show the children the backs of quarters to see the eagle with the olive branch and arrows.

Ask the children how they are like eagles. Then read Isaiah 40:30, 31 together. Focus the children's attention on the promise that believers can soar like eagles. God will be their strength if they trust him.

The flag of the United States of America

red stripes • courage
Joshua 1:7-9 • 1 Corinthians 16:13 • Hebrews 3:6

white stripes • purity
Psalm 51:10 • Matthew 5:8

blue • perseverance
Romans 5:3-5 • Hebrews 12:1-3 • James 1:2-4

The Christian Flag

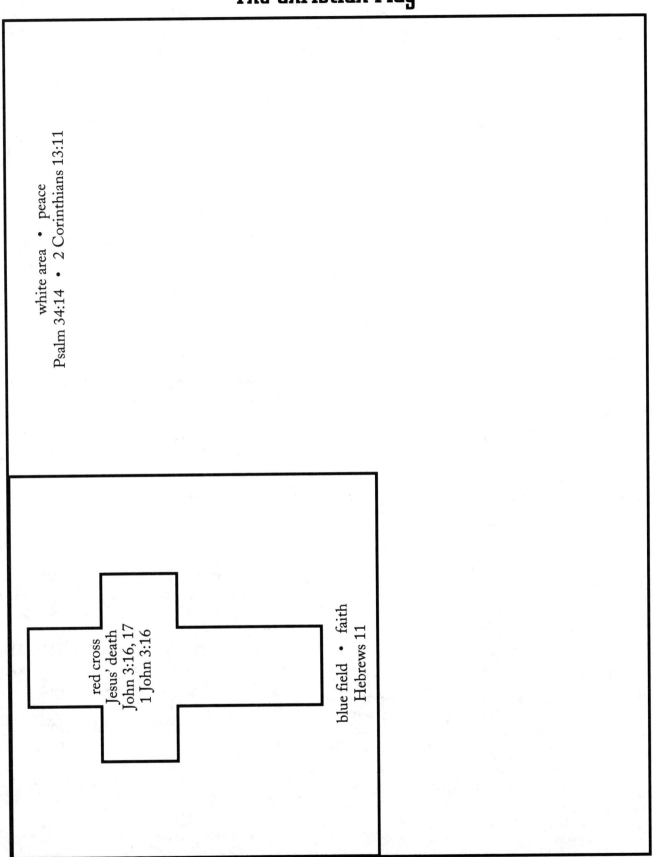

white area • peace
Psalm 34:14 • 2 Corinthians 13:11

red cross
Jesus' death
John 3:16, 17
1 John 3:16

blue field • faith
Hebrews 11

Design a flag

When the Israelites were wandering in the wilderness, the twelve tribes carried banners that identified the tribes. When in war, banners often identified the various regiments of the armies.

The word banner was used in another way in the Old Testament. It refers to a sign or a signal flag that would call the Israelites together. This is what Isaiah was talking about when he said the Messiah will stand as a banner (Isaiah 11:10).

Encourage each child to design a flag to represent his relationship with God. The children can use felt and craft glue to construct their flags. Guide the children to think of several shapes that could represent a relationship with God. For example, a heart could represent the love God has for us and we have for God. A cross could be a symbol for Jesus' death. A butterfly could represent the new life God gives to believers.

Have the children draw their flag designs on paper, cut out the pieces, and then use those paper shapes as patterns when cutting the felt. The flags can be glued to dowel rods and displayed in flower pots, vases, or on the walls.

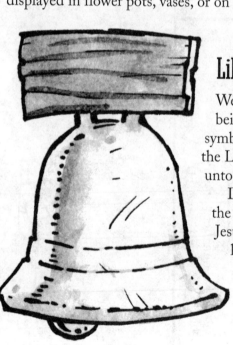

Liberty

Webster's definition of liberty is "the quality or state of being free." The Liberty Bell in Philadelphia has become a symbol of freedom in America. Leviticus 25:10 is printed on the Liberty Bell: "proclaim liberty throughout all of the land unto all the inhabitants thereof."

Discuss the meaning of liberty with the children. Focus the children's attention on how they are free because of Jesus. They are free from the bondage of sin. They can look forward to eternal life.

Discuss the importance of the children proclaiming liberty that is found in God. Encourage the children to brainstorm and carry out one way to proclaim this liberty.

Telling the truth

Focus the children's attention on the importance of telling the truth as you retell the familiar American folk tale about George Washington and his father's favorite cherry tree. George cut the cherry tree down one day. His father asked, "Who cut down my tree?" George refused to tell a lie for what he had done.

Discuss why trust may have been important during George Washington's term as president. Help the children understand how lying breaks down trust.

Jesus' tombstone

The tomb of the unknown soldier in Arlington Cemetery, Washington, D.C., has an inscription that reads "Here Rests in Honored Glory an American." Discuss with the children the significance of the tomb of the unknown soldier. It was dedicated to remember the soldiers who die in battle that are never identified.

Guide the children to write epitaphs for Jesus' headstone. For example, "Jesus does not 'rest in peace.' He reigns in victory over sin and death."

Sparklers

Give each child a sparkler. Discuss what happens when the sparkler is lit: sparks fly and the sparkler gives off light, yet in a few seconds it is extinguished. Ask: How is this similar to Jesus in our lives? How is this different? Light the sparklers. When they have burned out, pray together, thanking God for the eternal light he is in your lives.

Labor Day is a holiday to celebrate hard-working people and say good-bye to summer. Labor Day was first observed on September 5, 1882, in New York City. Large groups of laborers—mainly labor union members like bricklayers, machinists, and carpenters—celebrated the day with a big parade, picnics, and fireworks. They also had speeches about making working conditions better. Back then, people worked as much as twelve, fourteen, or even sixteen hours a day in unsafe conditions for very little pay. The Labor Day festival helped bring attention to these problems.

Today, this national holiday celebrates the hard work and dedication of all workers. People have the entire day to do whatever they want to do with their families and friends. It's also a great time to have one last weekend of summer fun before we settle in to our work or school schedules.

Devotion

Read Matthew 9:35-38 with the children. Ask these questions:

▶ What is the harvest Jesus is talking about?

▶ What work did Jesus do?

▶ What work can we do for Jesus to help with the harvest?

Talk about the different kinds of work we can do in the "harvest field." Then pray to God, asking him to send more workers to help with the harvest.

Prayer ideas

▶ Thank God for work.

▶ Thank God for rest.

▶ Praise God for creating our bodies for work and for rest.

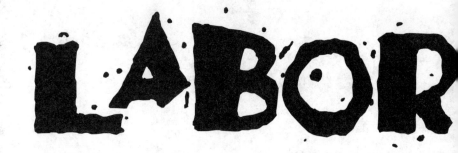

LABOR

JOBS IN THE BIBLE

There are many types of work and trades mentioned in the Bible. Here is a list of some of the jobs and the people who had those occupations.

Encourage the children to look up the people and jobs in a concordance and Bible dictionary to learn more about these biblical occupations.

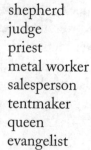

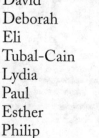

doctor	Luke
hunter	Esau
military leader	Joshua, David
tax collector	Matthew, Zaccheus
fisherman	Peter, James, John
preacher	Paul, Barnabas
writer	Matthew, Mark, Luke, John, Paul
shepherd	David
judge	Deborah
priest	Eli
metal worker	Tubal-Cain
salesperson	Lydia
tentmaker	Paul
queen	Esther
evangelist	Philip
king	Saul, David, Solomon, Herod
prophet	Elijah, Jeremiah, Isaiah
tanner	Simon
carpenter	Joseph
farmer	Cain, Abel, Gideon
musician	David
seamstress	Dorcas

DAY

KIDS' JOBS

Focus the children's attention on their jobs. They may say they do not have jobs. However they have some very important jobs with great responsibilities: student, son or daughter, brother or sister, and friend.

Discuss what their responsibilities are at each of these "jobs," the benefits, and when they have time off from their jobs. Help the children come up with some ways that they can do these "jobs" for God.

ETHICS AT WORK

This is a great time of year to teach about work ethics. Discuss with the children the importance of integrity in the workplace. Give them examples from your career or someone that they know.

Then discuss work ethics in the type of work they do: homework and jobs around the house. Discuss being reliable and doing a thorough job.

HOMEWORK ASSIGNMENT NOTEBOOKS

Guide the children to add Scriptures and phrases about work and rest to their homework calendars. You can purchase homework assignment notebooks in the stationery department of most discount stores. Help the children add Scriptures and special words of encouragement to various pages throughout the notebook. As the children get to those pages during the school year, they will recall what they have learned about work and rest.

Some suggested Scriptures:
- Genesis 2:2, 3
- Haggai 2:4
- Colossians 3:23
- Exodus 20:8-11
- Matthew 11:28, 29
- 2 Timothy 2:15

SCRIPTURE STICKERS

What you need
old magazines
scissors
permanent markers
plastic food wrap
gelatin
boiling water
paintbrushes

What you do
Help the children design stickers to remind them of what they have learned about work and rest. Help them cut out simple sticker-sized shapes from pages of the magazines. They could use pictures or just find colorful pieces to use as the background for the stickers.

The children will then write portions of Scriptures about work or rest on each sticker. Permanent markers work well on slick magazine paper.

Mix the gelatin powder with an equal amount of boiling water. Stir until the powder is dissolved. Have the children put their stickers facedown on plastic food wrap and brush the backs with the gelatin solution. Let dry.

The children can lick the backs of their stickers and stick them on their notebooks, lockers, jewelry boxes, and backpacks to remind them about work and rest.

Some suggested Scriptures:
◆ Genesis 2:2, 3   ◆ Exodus 20:8-11
◆ Haggai 2:4   ◆ Colossians 3:23
◆ 2 Timothy 2:15

SPIRITUAL REST

Read Matthew 11:28, 29 together and then discuss spiritual rest using these questions to focus your conversation.

◆ How does Jesus give us rest?
◆ When are people "weary and burdened"?
◆ What is "rest for your souls"?

REST

When God created the world, he rested on the seventh day. Could this have been the first Labor Day? Read Genesis 2:2, 3 together. Rest is important because it helps us to stay healthy. God designed our bodies to work and then rest.

God felt that rest was important enough to include it in the Ten Commandments. Read Exodus 20:8-11.

Guide children to pick one way to rest on each Sunday with their families. They could play a game, watch a movie, go for a walk, or take a nap. Encourage the children to make this part of their Sunday routine.

HONOR GOD'S LABORERS

To celebrate Labor Day, honor your congregation's ministers and staff. They are hard-working people on God's day of rest.

Help the children organize a way to give them some rest. They could plan a mini-vacation or retreat even for only a few hours. The children could solicit donations for an overnight stay at a nice hotel with a pool.

The children could pack a picnic lunch, complete with music and a blanket, and surprise the church staff during the Sunday morning service on Labor Day weekend.

Tell the children what your ideas are and let them brainstorm. They'll enjoy planning a surprise for the ministers and support staff.

History

Halloween traditions probably started in Britain and Ireland during the Celtic New Year on October 31. Halloween was first observed as an ancient festival to appease the forces of evil so that they would send the sun back in the spring after a long winter. As the days got shorter in the fall, the people feared the sun they worshiped would be killed by the evil forces of darkness. The people wore costumes to hide from these evil spirits. Some even disguised themselves as evil spirits to confuse the "real" ones. Little did these people know that toward the end of December, the days would once again begin to get longer and the sun would return. The Celts burned some of their crops, animals, and sometimes even people in large bonfires as part of their ritual. Once the days grew longer, they believed their sacrifices to the forces of evil had been successful.

In the ninth century, a Christian holy day called All Saints' Day was observed on November 1. It was a celebration to honor the saints and martyrs of the church. The night before All Saints' Day was known as All Hallows' E'en. A *hallow* meant a holy person. *E'en* was evening. This is where we get the word *Halloween*.

Like many holidays, Halloween has pagan origins. Because of its association with the spirit world, demons, evil spirits, and sorcery, it is especially important to understand Halloween's heritage in order to celebrate the holiday in a biblically appropriate way.

Did you know ...
. . . trick or treating comes from an old Irish custom? Beggars used to go to rich people's houses on October 31 and ask for gifts. They said the gifts were for a god who would destroy the houses of those who were not generous.

Prayer ideas

▶ Renew allegiance to God through Jesus Christ.

▶ Praise God for the victory over sin Jesus won on the cross.

▶ Thank God for the armor he has provided against Satan.

▶ Bind Satan from gaining any territory in God's battle for souls.

▶ Pray for courage and strength to battle temptation.

Light in the darkness

Give each child a candle in a votive candle holder. Read and discuss Colossians 1:13, 14. Discuss the light Jesus brings to this world darkened by sin. Light the candles as a reminder that light breaks through the darkness.

een

Flash dance

Halloween is often celebrated as a dark holiday. As believers, celebrate the light of Jesus in your lives.

Guide the children to choreograph a praise song using flashlights. Each child can hold a flashlight in each hand. The children can make up motions to the song. Then turn the lights out and sing the song several times as everyone does the motions.

Here are some songs using the word *light*.
- "This Little Light of Mine" (Traditional)
- "Shine, Jesus, Shine" (Graham Kendrick, MakeWay Music)
- "We Are the Light" (Tom McClain, Lillenas)
- "Let Your Light Shine" (Robert C. Evans, Integrity)
- "You Are the Light of My Soul" (Deborah A. Lambert, Integrity)

All Saints' Day

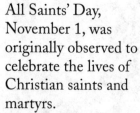

All Saints' Day, November 1, was originally observed to celebrate the lives of Christian saints and martyrs.

Give each child a votive candle in a candle holder. Read about and discuss various biblical characters. Honor these men and women by lighting a candle for each of them. Let the candles burn throughout the evening.

Saints of today

Help the children celebrate godly men and women they know. Encourage the children to write letters or make simple cassettes or video recordings telling the people how much they appreciate their stand for God.

Hall of Faith

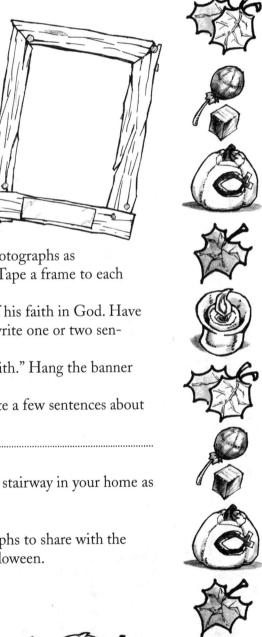

Guide the children to develop a Hall of Faith honoring godly people. Help the children make a list of people to be included in their Hall of Faith. Read Hebrews 11 for some ideas of people from the Bible. Think of some historical figures like Abraham Lincoln, Thomas Jefferson, Martin Luther King, Jr. Also help them add people like Corrie Ten Boom and Billy Graham. The children will also be able to think of some people in their own communities, churches, and families to add to their list.

Make plenty of photocopies of page 80. Find photographs of the people on the Hall of Faith list. Look in Bible dictionaries, encyclopedias, history books, and children's books. You may need to make a trip to the library to gather all of the photographs. Using a photocopier, reduce and enlarge the photographs as necessary to fit in the frame area on the photocopies of page 80. Tape a frame to each photograph. Make one page per person.

Each person has accomplished something in his life because of his faith in God. Have the children fill in the blanks, "By faith, ..." The children can write one or two sentences about the person below each photograph.

Have the children make a big banner with the title "Hall of Faith." Hang the banner with each person's photograph in a hallway.

Have the children make pages with their photographs and write a few sentences about their faith. Their photos can be added to the Hall of Faith also.

 Hang the banner and photographs in a hallway or down a stairway in your home as part of your Halloween decorations.

 Make a bulletin board using the banner and photographs to share with the whole congregation the Sundays before and after Halloween.

By faith

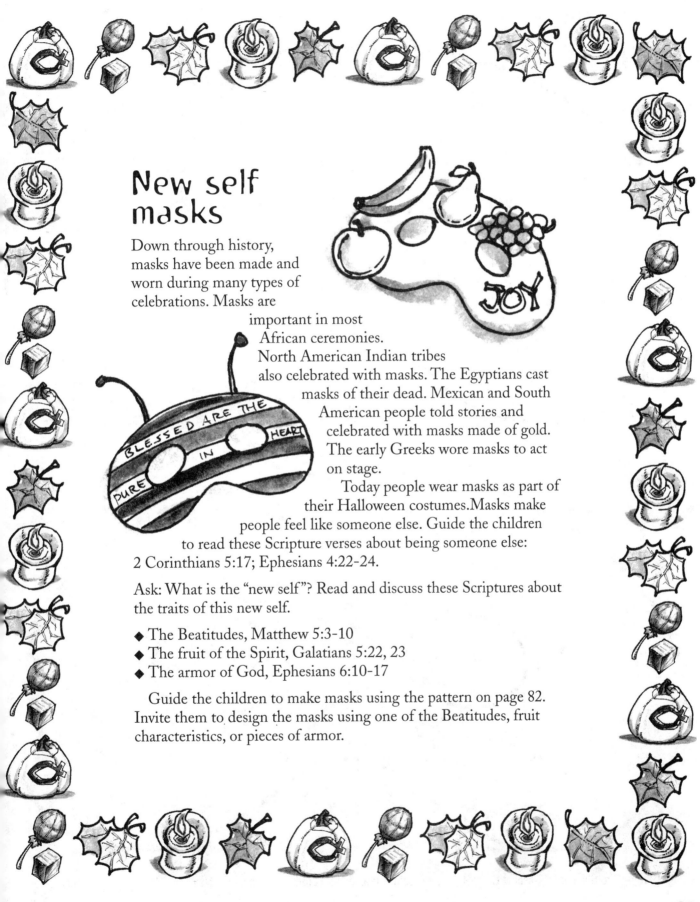

New self masks

Down through history, masks have been made and worn during many types of celebrations. Masks are important in most African ceremonies. North American Indian tribes also celebrated with masks. The Egyptians cast masks of their dead. Mexican and South American people told stories and celebrated with masks made of gold. The early Greeks wore masks to act on stage.

Today people wear masks as part of their Halloween costumes. Masks make people feel like someone else. Guide the children to read these Scripture verses about being someone else: 2 Corinthians 5:17; Ephesians 4:22-24.

Ask: What is the "new self"? Read and discuss these Scriptures about the traits of this new self.

- ◆ The Beatitudes, Matthew 5:3-10
- ◆ The fruit of the Spirit, Galatians 5:22, 23
- ◆ The armor of God, Ephesians 6:10-17

Guide the children to make masks using the pattern on page 82. Invite them to design the masks using one of the Beatitudes, fruit characteristics, or pieces of armor.

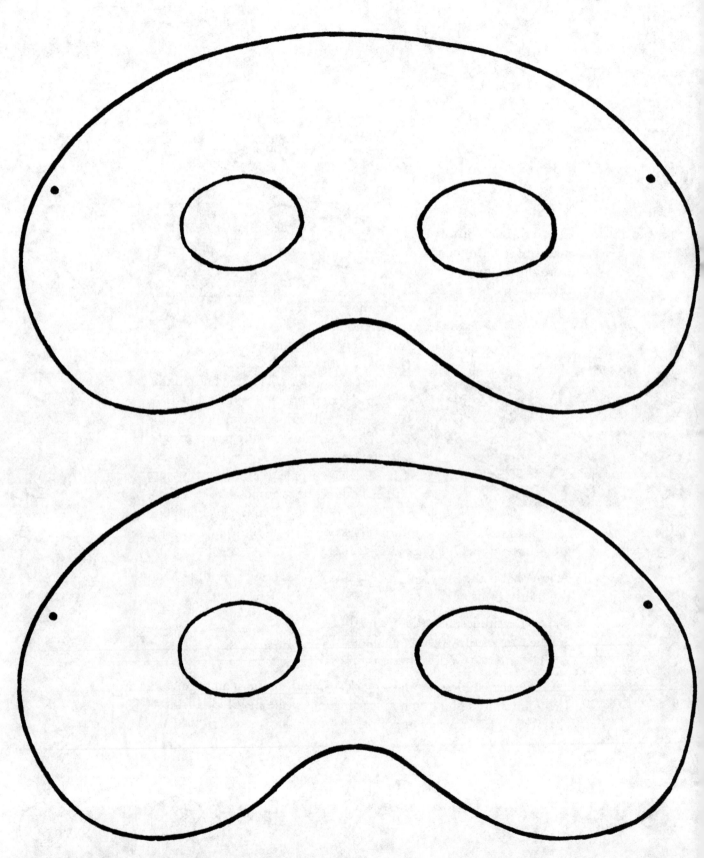

Pumpkin seeds

This tasty treat can be used to illustrate the parable of the sower or the parable of the weeds as found in Matthew 13. Talk about how seeds need light and good soil in order to grow. Jesus is the light that helps the seeds, the children of God, grow.

What you need
pumpkin seeds
paper towel
cooking spray, oil, margarine, or olive oil
salt
steamer
saucepan
baking sheet

What you do
Wash the seeds. Steam the seeds in a saucepan with a steamer for 30 minutes. This will soften the outside part of the seed. Add water to the saucepan as necessary. Remove the seeds from the saucepan and pat dry with a paper towel. Spread the seeds on a baking sheet. Spritz with cooking spray, oil, margarine, or olive oil until the seeds are shiny. Sprinkle with salt and stir. Bake the seeds at 300° for 30 minutes or until golden brown.

History

The most famous Thanksgiving celebration was in Plymouth, Massachusetts, in 1621. The colonists celebrated their first year in a new land and a successful harvest for their first growing season. They were thankful. Governor William Bradford led the people in celebrating with their Indian guests for three days.

This was not the first Thanksgiving festival, however. Thanksgiving services after the harvest were celebrated in other parts of the New World before 1621. The Pilgrims' families were the ones who carried on their first Thanksgiving tradition. This led to Thanksgiving being recognized years later as a national holiday.

Today, Thanksgiving is celebrated on the fourth Thursday of November with family reunions, big dinners, parades, special church services, and football games.

Devotion

Between Thanksgiving dinner and dessert, have someone read Psalm 100. Ask everyone to say one thing they are especially thankful for this year. Sing "Give Thanks" together.

Prayer ideas

▶ Thank God for family.

▶ Praise God for a year of his blessings and involvement in your lives.

▶ Thank God for the Pilgrim's faith.

▶ Thank God for at least five blessings in your life this year.

▶ Dedicate the Christmas season to God.

THANKSGIVING PLACE CARDS

Photocopy the place cards on page 91. Help the children color place cards for each person who will eat Thanksgiving dinner with them. They can add the names in large letters. The children will set place card at each person's place at the table.

THANKFUL PLACE MATS

What you need
colorful fall gift wrap
construction paper to coordinate with the gift wrap
scissors
pinking shears
markers
all-purpose glue

What you do
Cut a sheet of construction paper to 9" x 12" and a piece of gift wrap to 13" x 16". Use the pinking shears to cut the edges of the construction paper in a decorative shape. Glue the construction paper to the center of the colored side of the gift wrap.

GIVING

Cut another piece of gift wrap in a simple thanksgiving shape: leaf, pumpkin, apple, turkey, corn, pilgrim hat, handprint with fingers together as in prayer. This shape needs to be 3″ x 3″. Glue the left and right edges of the shape to the place mat at the napkin position. Raise the center of the shape a bit on the place mat in order to slide a napkin under it when dry.

The children can add Scripture verses or phrases to the place mats. They could also draw pictures and write each person's name on the place mats. Then, at the Thanksgiving meal, have people read or respond to the verses on their place mats.

Thanksgiving Scripture verses:
◆ Psalm 7:17
◆ Psalm 50:14
◆ Psalm 100
◆ Psalm 136:1
◆ 1 Corinthians 15:57
◆ Philippians 1:3

THANKFULNESS CALENDAR

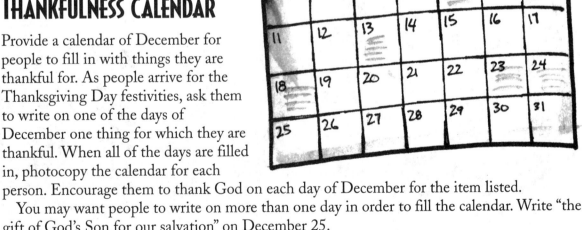

Provide a calendar of December for people to fill in with things they are thankful for. As people arrive for the Thanksgiving Day festivities, ask them to write on one of the days of December one thing for which they are thankful. When all of the days are filled in, photocopy the calendar for each person. Encourage them to thank God on each day of December for the item listed.

You may want people to write on more than one day in order to fill the calendar. Write "the gift of God's Son for our salvation" on December 25.

THANK-YOU NOTES

Invite the children to write simple notes of appreciation to their family members. They could tell them the things they like best about them, remind them of favorite times they spent with them, and tell them how much they love them. Encourage the children to place these notes in decorated envelopes on the Thanksgiving dinner plates.

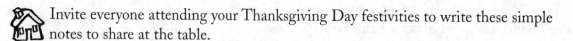

Invite everyone attending your Thanksgiving Day festivities to write these simple notes to share at the table.

THANKSGIVING SERVICE PROJECTS

Encourage the children to thank God for what they have by sharing with others. Here are some ideas for ways to give at Thanksgiving time.

FOOD PANTRY

Help children gather money for a food drive. Take the children on a grocery store shopping trip the weekend before Thanksgiving. Coach them as they buy food to donate to a food pantry.

The children could make posters advertising a food drive in their church or community the month of November. Have the children gather nonperishable staples to be donated to a food pantry.

THANKSGIVING DINNER

Help the children go to the grocery store and buy Thanksgiving dinner ingredients to give a family who may not be able to celebrate Thanksgiving with a big meal. Buy a turkey, several cans of vegetables, a box of stuffing, instant potatoes, a gravy mix, cranberry sauce, a loaf of bread, and a pie. Add the ingredients for a food item that may be a Thanksgiving tradition in your area.

Encourage the children to make cards with Thanksgiving greetings and a Scripture verse to send with the food. Help the children deliver the food to a shelter, food center, or government agency a few days before Thanksgiving.

CLOTHES PANTRY

Help the children gather, clean, and press clothes to be donated to a clothes pantry. The children could advertise at church and in the community. Guide them as they set up a drop-off site. This could be the beginning of a clothes pantry at your local congregation or mission.

THANKSGIVING DINNER GUEST

For Thanksgiving dinner, invite someone who might otherwise be alone on Thanksgiving Day. The children could make an invitation and mail it two weeks before. They could go with an adult to pick the person up on Thanksgiving Day. Inviting a different person every year may become a Thanksgiving tradition.

THANKSGIVING CROQUET

The Pilgrims did not play football as part of their first Thanksgiving celebration. However, they probably did play stoolball, a game very similar to croquet played with a soft ball.

Croquet is typically a summer game played outside on the lawn. Play this indoor variation as part of a Thanksgiving celebration.

What you need
adhesive address labels
croquet wickets or shoe boxes and scissors
croquet mallets or yardsticks
plastic foam, wood, or cork
foam ball or sock, cotton batting, thread, and needle

What you do
Write these sentences on adhesive address labels.

- Name one tangible thing you are thankful for.
- Name one tangible thing you are thankful for.
- Name one intangible thing you are thankful for.
- Name one intangible thing you are thankful for.
- Tell someone why you are thankful for them.
- Read Philippians 1:3 to someone and add "because. . . ."
- Read Psalm 7:17 aloud.
- Read 1 Corinthians 15:57 aloud.
- Name one reason you are thankful you know God.
- Name one reason you are thankful you are alive today.

Attach one label to each wicket. Attach small squares of foam, wood, or cork to the ends of the croquet wickets so the wickets will be able to stand on the floor.

If you do not have a croquet set, use shoe boxes to make wickets. Cut an open shoe box in half widthwise. Cut off the bottom of each half so you have two U shapes. Stand the U shapes upside down.

Use a foam ball or make a ball by stuffing the toe of a sock with cotton batting and sewing it closed. Use the croquet set mallets or yardsticks.

Set up a course inside. The children take turns hitting the ball. when the ball passes through a wicket, the child reads the direction from the wicket label and does what it says. Play continues to the next child according to croquet rules. Play is over when everyone has completed the course. There are no winners or losers.

Use a family room or garage for the course.

 Use a hallway or gym for the course.

CORNUCOPIA

Make this cornucopia to use as a centerpiece for the Thanksgiving table. Before dinner, have each person write a note of gratitude to God and place it inside the cornucopia. After dinner, each person can pull out a note and read it aloud as a Thanksgiving prayer.

What you need
3 cans refrigerated breadstick dough
1 egg
1 tablespoon water
heavy-duty aluminum foil
transparent tape
regular aluminum foil
nonstick cooking spray
large cookie sheet

What you do
Fold a 30″ x 18″ sheet of heavy-duty aluminum foil in half to 18″ x 15″. Roll diagonally to form a hollow cone about 18″ long with a diameter of 5″ at the wide end. Secure the ends with transparent tape. Stuff the cone with crumpled foil until it is rigid. Bend the tail of the cone to the desired shape for the cornucopia. Spray the outside of the cone with nonstick cooking spray. Place the cone on a large greased cookie sheet.

Mix the egg and water to make a glaze.

Open, unroll, and separate the breadsticks. Wrap one breadstick around the tip of the aluminum foil cone. Brush the end of the breadstick with the glaze, overlap the next breadstick about an inch, and press to attach. Continue wrapping the cone with the breadsticks, slightly overlapping the dough with all but three of the breadsticks.

Braid the remaining breadsticks. Brush the glaze on the dough around the mouth of the cone. Gently press on the braid. Brush the entire cornucopia with the glaze.

Bake at 350° for 45 minutes until the bread is light brown. If parts of the cornucopia darken early, cover them with pieces of aluminum foil.

Remove from the oven and let cool completely before removing the foil form.

COOKIE TURKEYS

This simple treat can be made by the children and used to decorate the Thanksgiving dinner table.

What you need
4 tablespoons margarine
10 ounces regular marshmallows or 4 cups miniature marshmallows
6 cups Rice Krispies cereal
chocolate sandwich cookies
chocolate frosting
candy corn

What you do
Melt margarine in a large saucepan over low heat. Add the marshmallows and stir until completely melted. Remove from heat. Add the cereal and stir until it is well-coated. Cool the mixture for 10 minutes. Grease hands and shape the mixture into 1 1/2" balls.

Twist apart the sandwich cookies. Add chocolate frosting to the inside of each half.

Press three candy corns into the frosting on half of the cookie halves in a fan shape. Press a cereal ball into the other half of the cookie halves.

Press each cookie half with the candy corn on the side of a cereal ball perpendicular to its other cookie half. To make the turkey's head, put a small amount of frosting on one candy corn and attach it to the cereal ball.

HAPPY THANKSGIVING

"Give thanks to the Lord, for he is good. His love endures forever." Psalm 136:1

HAPPY THANKSGIVING

"Give thanks to the Lord, for he is good. His love endures forever." Psalm 136:1

Advent

A dvent is designed to help people prepare their hearts for Christmas. The four Sundays before December 25 are the Sundays of Advent when people celebrate Jesus' first coming as a baby and his second coming as a king. The word *advent* comes from the Latin word *adventus* which means "a coming." Advent is a time of celebration for what God has done by sending Jesus to the earth, what he is doing in the church today, and what he will do when Jesus returns.

Advent is celebrated by lighting candles in an evergreen wreath, reading Scripture, praying, and singing Christmas hymns. Each Sunday centers around a particular theme.

The candle colors in the Advent wreath are symbolic: three purple for a penitent longing and one pink for joy. The pink candle is lit on the third Sunday to show anticipation for Jesus' coming. A tall, fat, white candle is placed in the center of the wreath. This is the Christ candle to be lit on Christmas day, celebrating the arrival of God's Son. Some families replace the three purple and one pink candles with white candles following Christmas day and burn those every day until Epiphany (January 6).

The circular shape of the Advent wreath represents God's unending love for us. The evergreen fronds represent eternal life.

Making an Advent wreath

Construct an Advent wreath by equally spacing one pink and three purple taper candles around an evergreen wreath. Position a large white candle in the center.

Use the Advent wreath as a centerpiece for the dining room table. Or place the Advent wreath on a skirted decorator table in the family or living room. Celebrate Advent with the family on Sunday afternoon or evening each week around the wreath.

Set up an Advent wreath in your classroom. Use the last few minutes of a class session each week to celebrate Advent together.

Photocopy the devotions on page 93 and use them as guidelines for your Advent observance. Let each person play a role in the Advent celebration. One person could read the Scripture. One person could pray. One person could light the candle.

ADVENT DEVOTIONS

Week 1
Prophecy

Read:
Isaiah 2:5; 9:2-6
Matthew 1:18-24
Luke 1:26-38

Ask:
- Why was Jesus' birth so important to the world?
- What was special about Jesus' birth?

Sing:
"O Come, O Come, Emmanuel"

Light a purple candle.

Pray:
Ask God to prepare you to celebrate his Son's birthday.

Week 2
Birth

Relight the first candle.

Read:
Luke 2:1-7

Ask:
- Where were you born?
- How do you think Mary and Joseph felt?

Sing:
"Away in a Manger"
"Silent Night"

Light the second purple candle.

Pray:
Thank God for the gift of salvation through Jesus.

Week 3
Shepherds

Relight the first and second candles.

Read:
Luke 2:8-20
Isaiah 52:7-10

Ask:
- Why do you think God included the shepherds in Jesus' birth?
- Why are you excited about Jesus' birth?

Sing:
"Angels We Have Heard on High"
"The First Noel"

Light the pink candle.

Pray:
Praise God for the message we have to share with others.

Week 4
Wise men

Relight the first three candles.

Read:
Matthew 2:1-11

Ask:
- What gift would you have given baby Jesus?
- What can you give Jesus?

Sing:
"O Little Town of Bethlehem"
"We Three Kings"

Light the third purple candle.

Pray:
Tell God what you want to give him this coming year.

December 25

Relight the four candles.

Read:
Luke 2:1-20

Ask:
- What is your favorite part of the Christmas story?
- Why is Jesus' birth important to you?

Sing:
"Joy to the World"
"O Come, All Ye Faithful"

Light the Christ candle.

Pray:
Thank God for his love shown by sending Jesus to the earth.

Christmas is the celebration when Jesus' birth is honored. No one knows exactly what day Jesus was born. But his birthday is celebrated on December 25. Gifts are given just like the wise men gave Jesus when he was a child.

Did you know . . .

. . . the first Christmas cards were sent in the early 1800's by English schoolboys wanting to show off their best writing to their parents?

. . . the first nativity scene was live, created by Saint Francis, who used an ox, a donkey, and his students?

. . . the legend of Santa Claus is probably based on the story of Saint Nicholas? Nicholas was a bishop in Turkey around A.D. 300. He devoted his life to giving to the hungry, homeless, and needy. He even secretly gave people money and gifts at night. Children in Holland called him Sinter Claes, from which then came the name, Santa Claus.

. . . decorated evergreen trees were originally a symbol of everlasting life? And one branch on the very top of an evergreen tree always points straight up—to God.

. . . "Silent Night" was composed in 1818 and first sung on Christmas Day?

. . . people put candle lights in their windows to remember Mary and Joseph looking for a place to stay in Bethlehem?

Christ

Christmas quiz

Help the children develop questions for a quiz on the biblical events surrounding Jesus' birth. They will enjoy quizzing their friends and family. Challenge them to include some tough questions like these.

- What Old Testament books prophesied Jesus' birth?
- How did Mary and Joseph get to Bethlehem?
- Did Mary ride a donkey to Bethlehem?
- Where did Mary and Joseph stay in Bethlehem?
- Did the angels sing or talk to the shepherds?
- Were the angels who visited the shepherds in the sky or on the ground?
- How many Magi were there?
- Where did the Magi visit Jesus?

Have your class prepare a quiz and give it to the school staff or an adult Sunday school class. They may be surprised at the adults' scores.

mas

Happy Birthday to Jesus!

One of the best ways for children to understand why we celebrate Christmas is to have a birthday celebration for Jesus. Help the children decorate a cake. Use some symbolic elements on the cake to represent Jesus' birth. Decorate the cake with yellow stars to remind them that Jesus was born in Bethlehem and a star led the Magi to Jesus. Add an angel figurine or ornament to the cake to remind them that the angels announced Jesus' birth. Add birthday candles to the cake and discuss how Jesus brought light to the world. Surround the cake with a length of evergreen garland to symbolize the eternal life they have through Jesus. Invite the children to light the candles, sing "Happy Birthday" to Jesus, and blow out the candles together.

Letterblankets

Letterblankets are Dutch pastries. Traditionally, the first letter of the guest's name is formed in the pastry and used to mark his place at the Christmas table. Help the children make this simple recipe, but make all Js to represent Jesus. Put one at each person's place at the table.

What you need

1 cup almond paste
1/4 cup sugar
1 large egg
pastry for two 9″ pie crusts
1 egg lightly beaten with 1 tablespoon milk
baking sheet
kitchen shears

What you do

Mix almond paste, sugar, and egg. Chill. Roll half of the pie pastry to about 1/4″ thickness and into a square shape. Using kitchen shears, cut out a J shape approximately 2″ wide and 7″ long. Lay the J on a lightly greased baking sheet. Press the marzipan (paste, sugar, egg mixture) on top of the letter, leaving a 1/2″ border on all sides. Roll and cut the remaining pastry the same way. Brush the border of the Js with the beaten egg. Place a second J over the marzipan and press the edges together to seal. Brush the surface with the egg glaze. Bake at 375° for 35 minutes until light brown.

Baby Jesus baby shower

Have a baby shower in honor of Jesus' birthday. Send baby shower invitations to the children. Invite them to bring a wrapped baby gift to give to a baby in Jesus' name. Use party supplies designed for a baby shower. Serve cake and punch and play baby shower games. Read about Jesus' birth from the Bible.

The children could make birth announcements announcing Jesus' birth. Show the children some examples of real birth announcements.

Tell the children at the party that they cannot give a gift to baby Jesus at the manger but they can give a baby gift that honors him. Have the children open their baby presents or have an adult designated to open the gifts. The adult could be a woman who is pregnant, dressed in a Bible-times costume. Once the gifts have been opened, guide the children to attach tags to the baby gifts that say, "Blessings to you in baby Jesus' name." After the party, give the gifts to a pregnancy help center, a women's shelter, or a missionary.

Gift tags

Guide the children to make gift tags with Scripture on them. The children can cut construction paper or gift paper in holiday shapes, like trees, canes, sleds, holly, bells, and candles. Then guide the children to write Scripture phrases on the tags along with "To" and "From." The children can add the gift tags to their packages when giving gifts.

Suggested Scripture verses:
- "For to us a child is born, to us a son is given." Isaiah 9:6
- "A Savior has been born to you; he is Christ the Lord." Luke 2:11
- "He gave his one and only Son." John 3:16

Scripture stars

An old German custom is to write Scripture verses on star-shaped paper and use the stars to decorate for the holidays. Help the children to cut stars from white construction paper. Have the children write on the stars one or more Scripture verses that they would like to memorize. Place the stars on an evergreen wreath. The children can work on memorizing the verses when they see the wreath hanging on the wall.

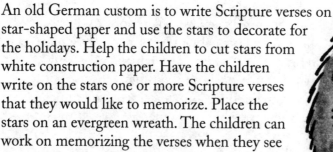

Hang the wreath over the kitchen table so that the family will see it during meals.

Christmas hymns

Choose one Christmas hymn to discuss with the children. Read all of the verses aloud. Discuss the hymn's primary focus. Have each person identify one phrase or line that has special meaning for them and tell why.

Suggested Christmas hymns:

"Come, Thou Long Expected Jesus"	"Infant Holy, Infant Lowly"
"O Come, O Come, Emmanuel"	"What Child Is This?"
"O Come, All Ye Faithful"	"I Wonder as I Wander"
"Joy to the World!"	"Go Tell It on the Mountain"
"Angels We Have Heard on High"	"Angels, From the Realms of Glory"
"The First Noel"	"While Shepherds Watched Their Flocks"
"It Came Upon the Midnight Clear"	"Away in the Manger"
"O Little Town of Bethlehem"	"Silent Night"
"Hark! the Herald Angels Sing"	"We Three Kings"
"How Great Our Joy!"	"Lo, How a Rose E'er Blooming"

Nativity character discussion

Give each person a figurine from the nativity scene and take turns telling something of significance about that person in the Christmas story or answer the question, "How would you tell the Christmas story from this person's point of view?"

 Use the nativity scene figurines as a centerpiece for a Christmas meal. Discuss each character between the meal and dessert.

God's special gift

Wrap the baby Jesus figurine from your nativity set. Add a gift tag that reads "To You" and "From God." Have the children open this gift together. Talk about the significance of Jesus' birth. Pray together, thanking God for sending his Son to the earth.

The Posadas

The Posadas is a Mexican Christmas tradition. Posadas means "lodging" and commemorates Mary and Joseph's search for a place to stay in Bethlehem.

Help the children celebrate their own adaptation of this Mexican tradition. Sometime after dark, give each child a lit candle or flashlight. Then have them line up and parade around the block or the outside of the building or house. Have the first three children carry the Mary, Joseph, and Jesus figures from the nativity scene. When the children return to the door, they will find the nativity scene outside. (You may need to get another adult to put the nativity scene in place so the children can be surprised.) They will place the figures in it. Lead everyone in singing "Away in a Manger" and "Joy to the World."

Luminarias

Luminarias are set out in some neighborhoods during the Christmas season. This holiday tradition was developed as a means of remembering Mary and Joseph's journey to Bethlehem. The luminarias can symbolize the lighting of the way for them to travel.

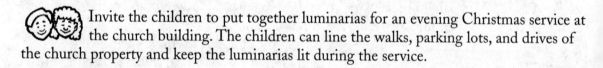

What you need
lunch sacks
sand
votive candles
matches

What you do
Fold the tops of the lunch sacks down to make a cuff so that they will stay open. Put sand in the lunch sacks to a depth of about 1". Place a votive candle in the sand of each sack. Line sidewalks and driveways with the sacks, spacing them about 4' apart. Light the candles at dusk and let them burn until they burn out.

....

Invite the children to put together luminarias for an evening Christmas service at the church building. The children can line the walks, parking lots, and drives of the church property and keep the luminarias lit during the service.

Walk-by nativity

Help the children plan a walk-by nativity in the church building on a Sunday morning in December. Designate children to be Mary, Joseph, and the shepherds. The children can plan where to put the nativity and how to decorate for it.

The nativity could be in the hallway or foyer of the church building. The children could staff it before and after the services.

....

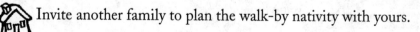

Invite another family to plan the walk-by nativity with yours.

Angels

Angels announced Jesus' birth to Joseph, Mary, and the shepherds. Talk with the children about other times in the Bible when angels appeared. Use a Bible concordance as necessary. Identify some significant elements of the appearances of God's messengers.

An extra chair

It is a tradition in Poland to add an extra chair for Jesus at the Christmas dinner table. Add this chair to your dinner table. Use the opportunity to discuss God's permanent presence with his people.

Christmas decorations

As you decorate, discuss with the children the meaning of your decorations. Especially point out the decorations that honor the true meaning of Christmas.

◆ Angels announced Jesus' birth.
◆ A star guided the wise men's search for Jesus.
◆ Lights can remind us that Jesus is the light of the world.

◆ Evergreen trees, wreaths, and garland are green throughout the year. This can represent the eternal life Jesus bought for us when he was crucified.

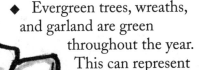

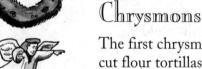

Chrysmons

The first chrysmons were Communion wafers cut into Christian symbols. Help the children cut flour tortillas into simple shapes like a cross, manger, star, or angel. Hang these chrysmons on a tabletop tree using nylon thread or fishing line.

Greeting card crafts

Recycle the Christmas greeting cards you receive for the next year. Enlist the children's help with preparing the cards for their new uses. Use one or more of these ideas.

Postcards

Cut off the fronts of the Christmas cards that are not embossed and do not have handwriting on them. Draw a line down the center of the back. Write a Christmas greeting on the left side, add an address and stamp, and send as postcards.

Note cards

Cut out the art designs on the Christmas cards. Glue them to blank note cards. Add glitter, beads, and other decorations. Write a Christmas greeting inside and send as Christmas cards. Family photos could be added to the front with the art glued around it.

Matching game

Cut the card fronts in half and use them as matching game pieces.

Place cards

Make simple place cards for the Christmas dinner table using art cut from Christmas cards. The children will enjoy finding just the right piece to glue on each place card.

Ornaments

Cut out art from Christmas card fronts and glue them to poster board. Trim the poster board around the art. Add glitter, glitter glue, beads, sequins, and pieces of ribbon, lace, and doilies. Phrases from Scripture verses could be added to the art or poster board. Punch a hole in the center top of each ornament and hang it on the Christmas tree or a wreath.

Jewelry

Make a pin to wear during the holidays. Cut out designs from a greeting card and glue it on poster board. Two or three art pieces can be overlapped to make a more intricate design. Trim the poster board. Glue a pin clasp to the back and put two to three coats of clear nail polish over the art. Decorate the pin with glitter, sequins, lace, or small beads.

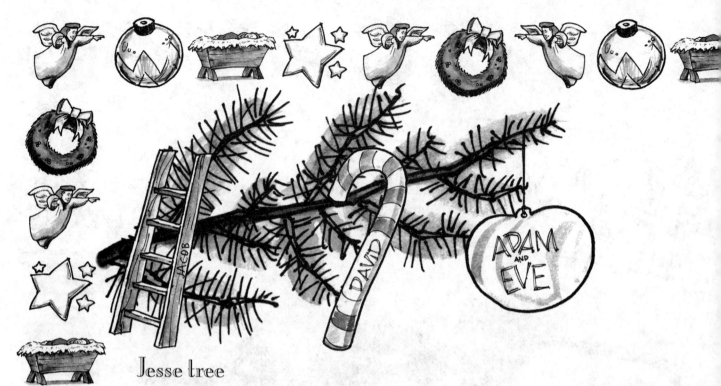

Jesse tree

The Jesse tree custom is based on a prophetic passage found in Isaiah 11. Read Isaiah 11:1-10. Jesse, King David's father, is part of Jesus' genealogy listed in Matthew 1:1-16. The Messiah was to come from the family of David.

The Jesse tree represents not only Jesus' family lineage but also God's covenant with the Israelite people. Each ornament on the Jesse tree represents an important biblical person who is in Jesus' earthly family or was an Israelite.

Making a Jesse tree

To set up a Jesse tree, use a small evergreen Christmas tree, a bare tree limb mounted in a can with plaster of paris, or a construction paper tree on a bulletin board. Place the tree where it will be seen often during the holiday season.

Add handmade or purchased ornaments that represent various people. These ornaments could be made from a variety of materials. Some ornaments could be cut from construction paper and decorated with markers, glitter, and ribbon. Several ornaments, Adam and Eve's apple, for example, could be purchased. The children could make some of the ornaments from clay or cinnamon dough.

Add communion wafers and cups to the Jesse tree to remember Jesus' gift of salvation. Add symbols to represent the Trinity: a dove for the Holy Spirit, a scroll to symbolize God's Word, etc. A six-pointed star—the star of David—could be added to the top of the tree. Include ornaments with some of the names of Jesus written on them. See the list on page 106.

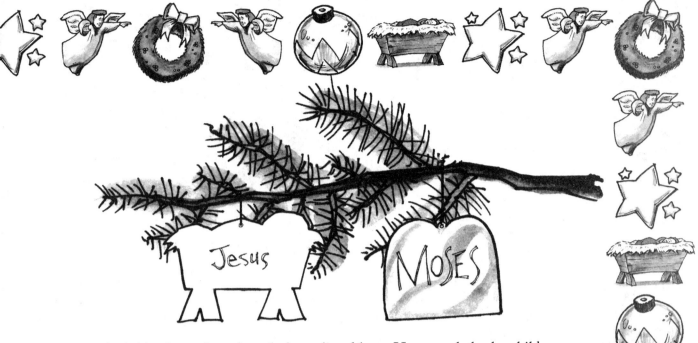

Several ideas for biblical people and symbols are listed here. However, help the children come up with their own list of names. Guide them to review familiar Bible stories and brainstorm an appropriate symbol for each person.

Person	Symbol
Adam and Eve	apple
Noah	ark, rainbow
Abraham and Sarah	tent
Isaac	altar with fire
Jacob	ladder from toothpicks
Joseph	colorful coat
Moses	tablets, burning bush
Boaz and Ruth	sheaf of wheat, suitcase
David and Bathsheba	shepherd's staff, crown, harp
Solomon	crown
Daniel	lion
Jonah	fish
Zechariah and Elizabeth	baby cradle
John the Baptist	honey pot
Joseph	hammer
Mary	baby in blanket, manger
Jesus	manger, crown

Make the Jesse tree an advent calendar by adding an ornament a day for the month of December.

Jesus' name ornaments

What you need
glass ornaments
permanent markers
Christmas ribbon

What you do
Help students look up the Scripture verses listed below and find the name for Jesus in each verse. Have the children write the names on the glass ornaments. They could write the Scripture references also. Help the children tie a ribbon bow around the top of each ornament. The ornaments could be hung on the Christmas tree or a tabletop tree.

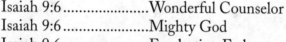

Isaiah 9:6 ....Wonderful Counselor
Isaiah 9:6 ....Mighty God
Isaiah 9:6 ....Everlasting Father
Isaiah 9:6 ....Prince of Peace
Matthew 1:23 ....Immanuel
Matthew 9:15 ....Bridegroom
Matthew 11:19 ....Son of Man
Mark 1:24 ....Holy One of God
Luke 2:11 ....Christ the Lord
John 1:29 ....Lamb of God
John 1:41 ....Messiah
John 1:49 ....Son of God
John 1:49 ....King of Israel
John 6:48 ....Bread of Life
John 10:7 ....Gate
John 10:11 ....Good Shepherd
John 11:25 ....Resurrection and Life
John 14:6 ....The Way, the Truth,
                                        and the Life
Acts 3:14 ....Holy and
                                        Righteous One
Romans 9:5 ....God
Romans 15:12 ....Root of Jesse

Ephesians 2:20 ....Chief Cornerstone
2 Thessalonians 3:16 ....Lord of Peace
Revelation 17:14...........Lord of Lords
Revelation 17:14...........King of Kings
Revelation 22:16...........Root and Offspring
                                        of David
Revelation 22:16...........Morning Star

An Easter reminder

Wrap a small box with large nails in it. When they have opened their gifts, open this small gift together. Continue to talk about the reason Jesus came to the earth as a man: to die for everyone's sins. Lead a prayer time, giving everyone an opportunity to thank God for the sacrifice of his Son.

The candy cane's story

The candy cane was originally created in order to remember the real meaning of Christmas: God's Son Jesus. A candy maker wanted his candy to tell the whole story of Jesus.

He used hard candy so that it would remind people that all of God's promises are solid, true, and reliable. The candy is white to represent the virgin birth and to symbolize Jesus' sinlessness.

The candy maker made the candy in the shape of a J to honor Jesus' name. The candy also looks like a shepherd's hook to recall that he is the Good Shepherd.

Real candy canes have three small stripes for the blood Jesus shed when he was beaten and scourged before he was crucified, and a big stripe for the blood Jesus shed on the cross for the sins of the world.

Using ornament hangers, hang candy canes upside down in the shape of a J on the Christmas tree.

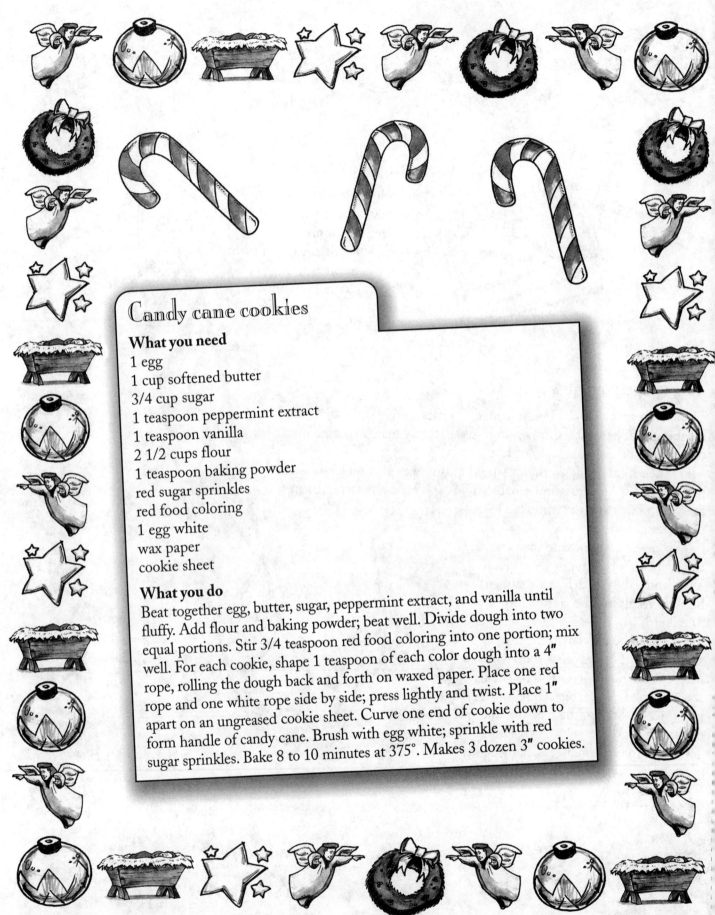

Candy cane cookies

What you need
1 egg
1 cup softened butter
3/4 cup sugar
1 teaspoon peppermint extract
1 teaspoon vanilla
2 1/2 cups flour
1 teaspoon baking powder
red sugar sprinkles
red food coloring
1 egg white
wax paper
cookie sheet

What you do
Beat together egg, butter, sugar, peppermint extract, and vanilla until fluffy. Add flour and baking powder; beat well. Divide dough into two equal portions. Stir 3/4 teaspoon red food coloring into one portion; mix well. For each cookie, shape 1 teaspoon of each color dough into a 4" rope, rolling the dough back and forth on waxed paper. Place one red rope and one white rope side by side; press lightly and twist. Place 1" apart on an ungreased cookie sheet. Curve one end of cookie down to form handle of candy cane. Brush with egg white; sprinkle with red sugar sprinkles. Bake 8 to 10 minutes at 375°. Makes 3 dozen 3" cookies.

Parties

He is Risen!

New Year's Party

Theme

Celebrate God's blessings and resolve to live for him in the coming year.

Invitations

See page 133. Add a little confetti to each envelope.

Decorations

Decorate for the party with several colors of helium balloons. If you plan to do the airmail balloon release suggested on page 15, fill enough balloons for each party attender to have one. Place the balloons various places around the room. For instance, you could tie the balloons to the handles of serving dishes or the necks of two-liter bottles.

Cover the serving tables with tablecloths and add purchased confetti. Also provide enough confetti for each party attender to throw at midnight.

By hand or computer make a banner that reads "Happy New Year" and add the year's date to it. Party attenders could color the banner with markers and hang it once they arrive.

Favors

Noisemakers

Write various Scripture verses on several types of paper noisemakers. Add curling ribbon streamers for pizzazz. Choose from these Scriptures.

- 2 Corinthians 5:17
- Romans 12:2
- Psalm 100:1
- Psalm 100:5
- Psalm 150:6

Party hats

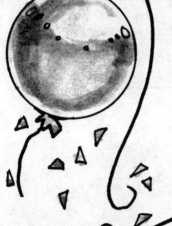

Add tissue paper streamers to the points of party hats. Write "The old has gone. The new has come. 2 Corinthians 5:17" on the hats with a permanent marker.

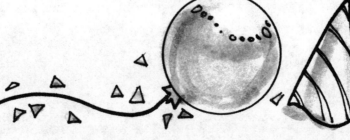

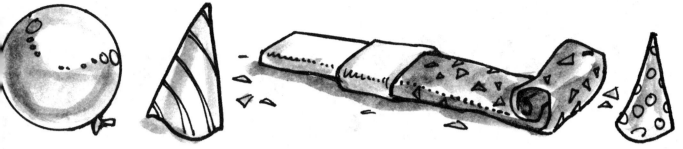

Food

Cookie of the month

Provide the following shaped cookie cutters or a shape that would represent that month.

January—snowman
February—heart
March—shamrock
April—cross

May—flower
June—butterfly
July—flag
August—schoolhouse

September—leaf
October—pumpkin
November—turkey
December—star

Using refrigerator cookie dough, have party attenders make cutout cookies to serve. The cookies can be frosted and then decorated with colored sugars, red hot cinnamon candies, sprinkles, coconut, candy, or gumdrops.

Activities

- ◆ Pick one of the New Year's resolution activities on pages 15-17 for the party attenders to complete during the party.
- ◆ Guide small groups of party attenders to prepare mumming skits as described on page 13. Have the groups present the skits during the party.

Video Idea

Make a short home video of the party attenders talking about their New Year's resolutions. Between each video clip, pan across a sign on a piece of poster board that reads "With God's help, I will succeed." Play the video during the devotion time.

Devotion

Ask each party attender to take a turn sharing a favorite memory from last year. Light candles and discuss hopes for the coming year as described on page 12. Read 2 Corinthians 5:17. Talk about how nothing can be changed about last year. However, the coming year can be molded. Discuss what God's goals, or his resolutions, may be for the party attenders. Complete the airmail balloon release as described on page 15.

Epiphany Party

Theme

Celebrate Jesus as King.

Invitations

See page 134. Glue glitter and sequins to the crown before mailing.

Decorations

Decorate with crowns and yellow crepe paper. Construct the crowns from poster board and cover them with foil gift wrap or aluminum foil. Place some of the crowns on the food table and hang some with the crepe paper. Set up a nativity scene in the room.

Favors

"Greatest gift" boxes

What you need
small jewelry gift boxes
all-purpose gift wrap
ribbons, bows, curling ribbon
scissors
transparent tape
gift tags or poster board cut to gift tag size
markers

What you do
Wrap and decorate an empty jewelry box for each party attender. Add a gift tag that reads: "Jesus is the greatest gift you will ever receive."

At the party, explain to the attenders that God gave a wonderful gift to the world—

Jesus. The party favors are to remind them of this gift. Tell them there is no reason to unwrap this small gift box because the gift of Jesus has already been given and unwrapped. All they have to do is accept it.

Food

Make the Epiphany cake described on page 18. Or make the bundt cake ahead of time and have the party attenders do the decorating. When the party attender finds the bean or prize, have some ideas for games to suggest.

Serve apples or a recipe that features apples. Tell about the apple's star as described on page 19. Several apple recipes are on pages 47-50.

Activities

◆ Include a simple gift exchange with the Epiphany party instead of a Christmas party.
◆ Include the "light of the world" candles described on page 19 in the devotion time.
◆ Make the potpourri sachet described on page 21. Each party attender could make two—one to keep and one to give as a gift.

Photo Idea

Rent an elaborate crown from a costume shop. Using a Polaroid camera, photograph each party attender holding the crown. Add this caption to the photographs: Jesus is the King in my life. The party attenders can take the photographs home.

Devotion

Sing a few of the worship choruses suggested on page 20. Read the story of Jesus' birth and the visit by the wise men found in Matthew 1:18—2:12. Discuss the wise men's visit to the King of kings. Ask: How was Jesus the King of kings? How did he show that he was King? Close with one of the prayer ideas from page 18.

Valentine's Day

Theme

Celebrate love for God and love for others.

Invitations

See page 135. Add color to the invitations with red and pink markers.

Decorations

Write some of the Valentine's Day Scriptures from page 29 on large hearts cut from red, pink, and white poster board. Hang the hearts from the ceiling with fishing line or nylon thread. During the party, party attenders can look up the Scriptures, read, and discuss their meanings.

Before the party, prepare the background for the bulletin board described on page 31. Have the party attenders write examples of love on heart-shaped doilies and add them to the bulletin board during the party.

Using a heart-shaped sponge and paints, stamp hearts on paper cups for refreshments.

Use paper doilies to decorate the tables and walls. Decorate with the colors red, white, and pink.

Favors

Soap valentines

Have the party attenders make the soap valentines described on page 27. Each party attender should make at least two of these favors—one to keep and one to give away. If there will not be enough time at the party for the attenders to make the soap valentines, make them ahead of time and give them as favors at the party.

Party

Food

Heart pizza

Order uncut pizzas. Use a heart-shaped cookie cutter to cut heart-shaped pieces for everyone. Or make pizzas from scratch. Form the dough into a heart shape, then add the pizza sauce, toppings, and cheese.

Activities

◆ Have the party attenders select a biblical character to model after as described on page 30. Have party attenders act out portions of each character's story for the other attenders.

◆ Party attenders could complete a simple service project as described on page 28. The project could be part of the party or completed just before or just after the party.

Devotion

Complete the conversation with God activity from page 28. Read and discuss John 3:16 and 1 John 3:16 as described on page 26. Conclude with a prayer time centered on thanking God for the love that he demonstrates to us—through his Son's death, our families and friends, having the Bible to read and guide our lives, the Holy Spirit's influence in our lives, and his promise of eternal life.

Easter Party

Theme

Celebrate Jesus' death on the cross for the world's sins and Jesus' resurrection from the dead.

Invitations

See page 136.

Decorations

Decorate the area for the party with the salvation colors: black, red, blue, white, green, and gold. You could use balloons, crepe paper, and colored partyware. Use eggs and crosses in your decorations. Refrain from using bunnies.

Add an Easter tree to your party decorations. The children could make ornaments during the party to add to the tree. See page 37 for instructions.

Make the Easter wreath described on page 36 and use it to decorate for the party. The party attenders could also make these wreaths at the party.

Favors

Use colored eggs as favors for the Easter party. Color several dozen eggs before the party. The party attenders can color eggs during the party as well. See pages 38-40 for some ideas. Use the eggs during the egg hunt.

Food

Easter recipes

Before or during the party, prepare any of these recipes.

- Easter prayer pretzels described on page 40
- Easter cupcakes described on page 42

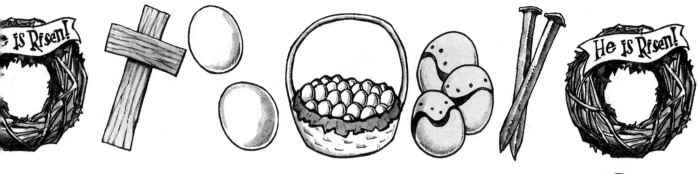

- Cross pretzels described on page 42
- Hot cross buns described on page 43
- Resurrection surprise rolls described on page 44

Easter punch

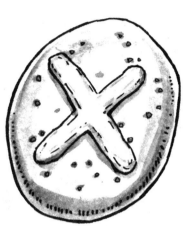

What you need:
4-ounce can frozen lemonade
2-liter bottle ginger ale
64 ounces cranberry juice
small plastic two-part eggs

What you do:
Mix all of the ingredients. Put the punch in a pretty punch bowl. Boil several two-part eggs to clean them. Float the eggs in the punch.

Activities

- Help the party attenders color eggs in the colors of salvation. This activity is described on page 38 and 39. Discuss the meanings of the various colors. This could be done during a specific devotion time near the end of the party.
- Color eggs with a resurrection message. Instructions are given on page 40. Give the party attenders several examples of resurrection messages, then let them think of their own.
- Provide two-part eggs with the resurrection symbols described on page 41. Have an Easter egg hunt using all of the eggs. The party attenders can gather the eggs in the baskets they brought with them to the party.

Devotion

Read 1 Peter 2:24. Discuss sin; define it if necessary. Guide the party attenders to hammer nails into a block of wood as described on page 34.

EARTH DAY

THEME

Celebrate God's creations and renew a commitment to take good care of God's earth.

INVITATIONS

See page 137.

DECORATIONS

Decorate for the party using earth shapes and the recycling triangle. Cut the shapes from poster board in various sizes. Add designs to the shapes using markers. The children can help with decorating the poster-board shapes. Tape to the walls of the room where the party will be held.

Use green plates, napkins, and cups for the party. When the party attenders have made the creation numbers described on page 46, have them add these to the party's decorations.

FAVORS

Choose one of the bird feeders on page 50 to have the party attenders make during the party. Provide the supplies or add a supply list to the invitations.

FOOD

In honor of Johnny Appleseed, prepare some of the apple recipes on pages 47-50. The party attenders may enjoy preparing the applesauce and apple soup recipes themselves.

PARTY

Use a large, round fish bowl to serve a simple punch. Decorate the fish bowl like a globe. Use craft paint in squeeze bottles to outline the continents. Then add craft paint to fill in the land and sea colors. When the paint is dry, spray the outside of the bowl with clear acrylic or polyurethane.

ACTIVITIES

◆ The party attenders could begin a recycling service project. Discuss a specific project at the party, assign jobs, and pass out any information. Follow up within a week to see how the party attenders are doing with their assignments. One service project idea is described on page 51.
◆ On the party invitations, tell the attenders to bring their recycling bins from home. Have them decorate the bins during the party as described on page 52.
◆ Gather old crayons before the party. During the party, have the party attenders melt and reshape these crayons. Once the crayons have cooled completely, have the party attenders make a poster featuring God's reasons for caring for the earth.

DEVOTION

Read Genesis 1:1—2:3. Discuss what God created on the various days. Guide the party attenders to draw or write on number cutouts what was created on each day. See page 46 for more information.

119

Prayer Party
A National Day of Prayer Celebration

Theme

Celebrate a personal relationship with God.

Invitations

See page 138.

Decorations

Decorate for the prayer party using triangles. A triangle reminds us of the Trinity—God the Father, God the Son, and God the Spirit. A relationship with each of these persons of the Godhead is important in the Christian life.

Cut triangles from colorful poster board. Hang them from the ceiling and tape them to the walls. String some of the triangles on yarn to make garlands.

Cut a large triangle from a corrugated cardboard appliance box. Tape it onto a doorframe and use it as a pass-through to the party.

Cut or fold paper napkins in half diagonally to form triangles. Draw triangles on plastic or paper cups with a permanent marker.

Favors

A Jewish tradition from the second century was to wear phylacteries on the forearm and forehead during prayer. Orthodox Jews continue this tradition today. The small boxes contained Scripture verses reminding the Jews that the laws of God were to be the center of their lives.

Give the party attenders baseball hats. Instruct them to write a Scripture inside the facing of the hat with a permanent marker. The Scripture could be one of their favorite verses or simply a verse about prayer.

The party attenders can wear the baseball hats during the party and take them home as reminders of the importance of prayer in their everyday lives.

Food

Prayer pretzels
Make the prayer pretzels described on page 40 during the party.

Popcorn prayer
Spread out a clean sheet on the floor. Put an airpop popcorn popper with the top off in the center of the sheet. Have the party attenders stand or sit around the perimeter of the sheet. Plug in and turn on the popper. As the corn pops out of the popper, the party attenders can shout to God something they are thankful for. When all the kernels have popped, enjoy picking up and eating the popcorn.

Activities

- Plan a prayer time moving from station to station as described on page 54. Divide the party attenders into groups of three.
- A progressive prayer walk could take place during the party. Plan to visit locations near where the party is being held. See page 55 for more details.
- Have the party attenders make prayer journals as described on page 56. Tell the attenders to bring family snapshots. Provide simple, inexpensive journals. Include a quiet time during the party for the attenders to pray through their journals for the first time.

Devotion

Read and discuss the Lord's Prayer found in Matthew 6:9-13. Use the information on page 57 to help in your devotion time.

Patriotic Party

Theme

Celebrate being an American.

Invitations

See page 139. Color the flag red and blue.

Decorations

Decorate for the party using red, white, and blue. Use balloons, crepe paper, various sizes of flags, and patriotic banners. Many red, white, and blue party supplies can be found at party goods stores.

Favors

Decorated T-shirts

Provide a T-shirt for each party attender. During the party, the attenders can decorate their own shirts. Provide fabric paint and flag iron-ons.

Food

All-American meal

Serve hot dogs, chips, apple pies, and Cokes.

Flag cake

Prepare a cake mix in a 9" x 13" baking pan. Frost the cake with white frosting. Arrange blueberries for the blue field and strawberry halves for the red stripes. Or use blue and red candy for the blue field and red stripes.

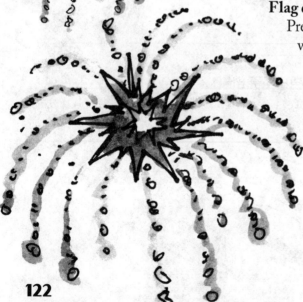

Activities

◆ Light sparklers and discuss Jesus' light in our lives. See page 71.

◆ Photocopy pages 68 and 69. Guide the party attenders to look up the Scripture references, discuss the various topics, and color the flags.

◆ Sing some of the party attenders' favorite patriotic songs.

◆ Discuss being an American. Use these questions to guide your discussion.
What is great about being an American?
What is your favorite thing about living in America?
What does America do well?
What could America do better?

Devotion

Discuss the seal of the United States and compare it to being like an eagle. Read Isaiah 40:30, 31. See page 67 for more information.

Light Party
A Halloween Experience

Theme

Celebrate the light of the world, Jesus.

Invitations

See page 140.

Decorations

Decorate for the light party using anything that gives off light—candles, flashlights, strings of Christmas lights, oil lamps.

Younger children could make candles by covering paper towel tubes with construction paper. Have them make a round base as a candle holder. Add a yellow and orange tissue paper flame.

Favors

Provide mini-flashlights or inexpensive flashlights from a discount store.

Give each party attender a votive candle and votive candle holder to use during the party and to take home as a reminder of Jesus' light in the world.

Food

Pumpkin seeds
During the party, the party attenders could make the pumpkin seeds described on page 83.

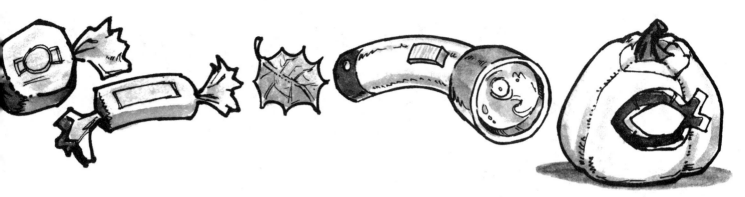

Candy

Provide plenty of individually wrapped Halloween-type candy. If the party attenders will not be trick or treating during this holiday season, provide enough candy for each child to take some home.

Activities

◆ Create a flash dance using flashlights and a few praise choruses. This activity is described on page 77.
◆ Make a Hall of Faith display as described on page 79. Leave the Hall of Faith up for a week after the party or move it to a wall in the church building for several weeks.
◆ Divide the party attenders into groups of three. Provide one pumpkin for each group to carve. The groups could carve Christian symbols like a cross or Icthus fish into the pumpkin. Or, after discussing several biblical characters, they could carve a shape representing one of the biblical characters.

Devotion

Read about and discuss various biblical characters. Then honor these men and women by lighting candles for each of them. See page 78 for more details about All Saints' Day.

Read Colossians 1:13, 14. Discuss the light Jesus brings to a world darkened by sin. Have each party attender light a candle in a votive candle holder as a reminder that light comes after darkness.

Thanksgiving Party

Theme

Celebrate God's provision with thankfulness.

Invitations

See page 141.

Decorations

Decorate with traditional Thanksgiving items—turkeys, pumpkins, corn husks, Indian corn, leaves. Use orange, brown, green, and yellow as the main colors for the party.

Favors

Place mats and place cards

Help the party attenders make the place mats or the place cards described on page 84. The place mats and place cards can be used for the party. Then the party attenders can take them home to use during their families' Thanksgiving festivities.

Food

Cookie turkeys

Provide the supplies to make the cookie turkeys described on page 90. The party attenders can assemble the cookies

during the party. Have each party attender make two: one to eat and one to take home.

Thanksgiving dinner

Serve Thanksgiving dinner with a twist. Make turkey sandwiches and cut them in fourths diagonally. Serve french fries and cheese for dipping. Purchase apple pies from a fast-food restaurant.

Activities

◆ Play a few rounds of indoor croquet. See page 88 for details of setting up the course with a Thanksgiving theme.

◆ Help the party attenders make thankfulness calendars for the month of December. See the directions for this activity on page 85.

◆ Organize the party attenders to show their thankfulness to God by completing a service project. The project could be carried out as part of the party or planned at the party and completed at a later date. Several ideas for service projects are listed on pages 86 and 87.

Devotion

Read Psalm 100 together. Ask the party attenders to say one thing for which they are especially thankful this year. Then sing "Give Thanks."

Christmas Party

Theme

Celebrate Jesus' birth, life, and death to save the world from sin.

Invitations

See page 142.

Decorations

Decorate with symbols that represent the true meaning of Christmas. Use angels, stars, lights, evergreen trees, wreaths, and garlands. See page 101 for more details.

Favors

Candy canes

Give each party attender a candy cane and tell the candy cane's story from page 107.

An Easter reminder

Give each party attender a small wrapped box with a large nail in it as a reminder of why Jesus came to the earth.

Food

Birthday cake for Jesus

Decorate a cake to celebrate Jesus' birthday. Bake the cake ahead of time and have the party attenders decorate it during the party. When it is time

for dessert, stand around the cake, sing "Happy Birthday" to Jesus, and blow out the candles together. See page 95 for details about decorating the cake.

Candy cane cookies
Have the party attenders help make candy cane-shaped cookies. See the recipe on page 108.

Letterblankets
Make letterblankets, a Dutch pastry, to be served at the party. The recipe is on page 96.

Activities

- Discuss each nativity scene character as described on page 99.
- Have a baby shower for baby Jesus. See page 97 for more information.
- Have the party attenders bring several used greeting cards. During the party, complete one of the crafts from page 102 or 103.

- Make the Jesus' name ornaments described on page 106. Donate the ornaments and a small tabletop tree to a retirement center, soup kitchen, or mission.
- Prepare a Christmas quiz for the party attenders to take. See page 94 for some suggested questions. Discuss each question once everyone has had a chance to record their answers.

Devotion

Read the Bible account of Jesus' birth in Luke 2:1-20. Discuss why Jesus came to the earth. Sing several Christmas hymns listed on page 98. Close with a prayer time thanking God for the sacrifice of his Son's life to save the world from sin.

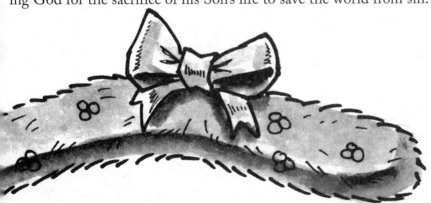

Invitations

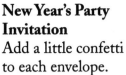

Epiphany Party Invitation

Glue glitter and sequins to the crown before mailing the invitations.

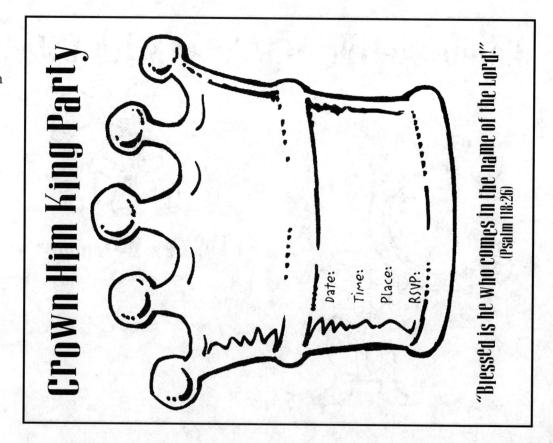

Crown Him King Party

Date:
Time:
Place:
RSVP:

"Blessed is he who comes in the name of the Lord!"
(Psalm 118:26)

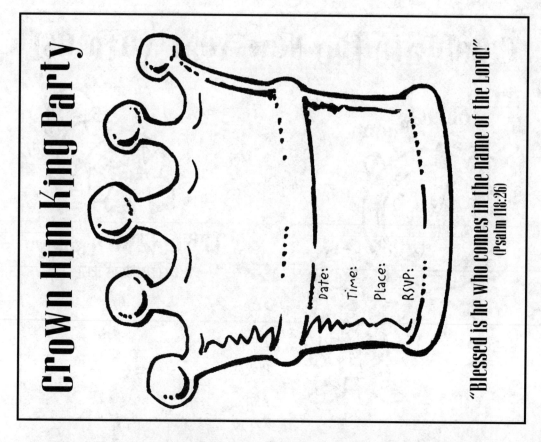

Crown Him King Party

Date:
Time:
Place:
RSVP:

"Blessed is he who comes in the name of the Lord!"
(Psalm 118:26)

**Valentine's Day
Party Invitation**
Add color to the
invitations using red
and pink markers.

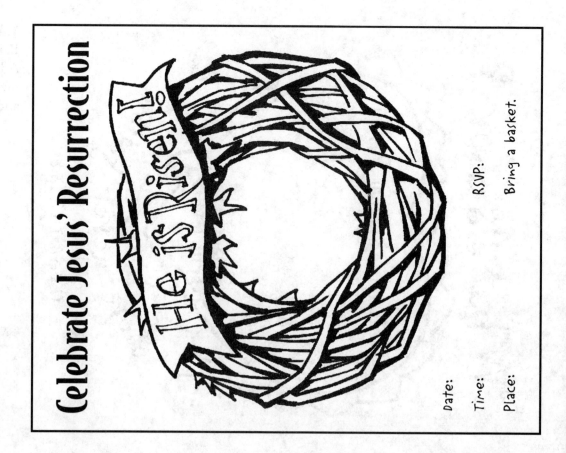

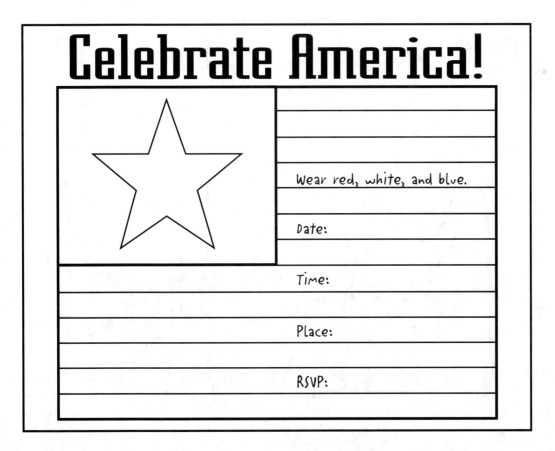

Celebrate America!

Wear red, white, and blue.

Date:

Time:

Place:

RSVP:

Patriotic Party Invitation
Color the flag red and blue.

Celebrate America!

Wear red, white, and blue.

Date:

Time:

Place:

RSVP:

Come and Celebrate Jesus the Light

Date:

Time:

Place:

RSVP:

Colossians 1:13, 14

Come and Celebrate Jesus the Light

Date:

Time:

Place:

RSVP:

Colossians 1:13, 14

GIVE THANKS

"GIVE THANKS TO THE LORD, FOR HE IS GOOD. HIS LOVE ENDURES FOREVER." PSALM 136:1

Date:

Time:

Place:

RSVP:

GIVE THANKS

"GIVE THANKS TO THE LORD, FOR HE IS GOOD. HIS LOVE ENDURES FOREVER." PSALM 136:1

Date:

Time:

Place:

RSVP:

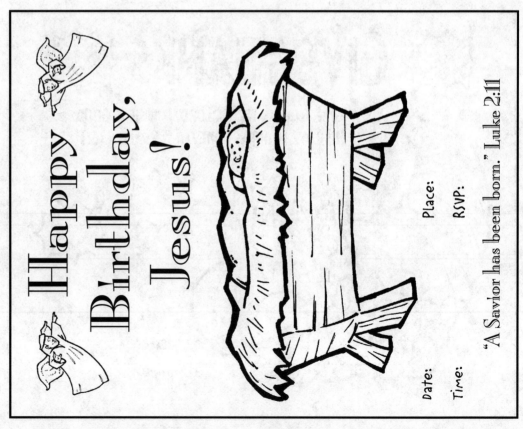

Celebrate!

Recipe Index

Celebrate!

Craft Index